All rights reserved; no part of this publication may be reproduced or transmitted by any means, electronic, mechanical, photocopying or otherwise, without the prior permission of the author.

First published in Great Britain in 2025

Ronee Hulk, 22a Annandale Street, Edinburgh, EH7 4AN, UNITED KINGDOM

Edited by J.Faulkner

Copyright © Text Ronee Hulk 2025

Copyright © Cover illustration Christopher Hewitt 2025

The moral right of the author has been asserted

A catalogue record of this book is available from the British Library

ISBN 978-1-83709-319-9 **Paperback**

ISBN 978-1-83709-320-5 **Hardback**

Printed and bound in Great Britain

10 9 8 7 6 5 4 2 1

WWW.RONEEHULK.COM

DEAR FUTURE:
YOU CAN KEEP THE CHANGE

RONEE HULK

"The real voyage of discovery consists not in seeking new landscapes but in having new eyes"

Marcel Proust.

Contents

Foreword: Before It's Too Late   9 - 15
It began with curiosity; we taught machines to think. Now, the student has learned too well. AI will upend every system we've built: work, relationships, wealth, purpose. Each will be unsettled. The question is: what does it leave still standing?

Introduction: Ghost in the Code   17 - 23
What is AI? Intelligence no longer sits in one place but moves through everything we touch. From machine learning and LLMs to AGI and ASI, let's untangle the acronyms, define the layers of intelligence we've built, and see how each fits into the larger story of machines that think.

1. Of Minds and Machines   25 - 31
From factory floors to living rooms, automation has become the heartbeat of a redundancy wave that will dismantle not just industries, but identities too. The machines aren't just coming for our jobs, they're coming for our relationship with work itself. When everything we do can be done better by code, what's left for us to do at all?

2. The Efficiency Trap   33 - 40
We built systems to make life smoother, faster, smarter. Efficiency was meant to free us, but instead it traps us in endless refinement, where purpose becomes process and meaning dissolves into data. We were promised freedom, but we've been delivered a cage. Is there any way out?

3. Behind the Curtain   41 - 44
Invisible code now conducts the orchestra of our lives, deciding what we see, hear, and believe. It selects our news, our feeds, even our outrage, shaping a world that feels chosen by us, but isn't. Algorithms have become the unseen guiding hand of modern thought; the question is no longer what we think, but who's doing the thinking.

4. The Cost of Perfect Health   45 - 53
Medicine promises lives that may stretch across centuries. Robots will run wards, algorithms will diagnose before symptoms appear, as precision health replaces human touch. We will save and extend more lives than ever before, but in doing so, will human compassion become the rarest treatment of all.

5. Chalkboards & Chatbots   55 - 63
Education stands on the brink of its greatest transformation. Personalised AI learning promises to optimise every lesson, every child and every outcome. It is the triumphant end of one-size-fits-all schooling and the dawn of lifelong, data-driven learning. But as machines take the lead in teaching us, is there an unseen cost?

6. The Price of Progress 65 - 72
Our art, music, and writing now share their canvas with algorithms that can imitate emotion. Ownership is uncertain, authorship contested, and the law still unwritten. In striving for perfection, will we erase the beautiful flaws that evidence and characterise our humanity?

7. Loneliness in the Age of Connection 73 - 79
Loneliness is the greatest irony of our hyper-connected age. Our devices listen, respond, and reassure, yet real connection is slipping further away. As robots become partners and digital beings care for our loved ones, we must ask: when affection can be automated, will love still mean anything at all?

8. The God Question 81 - 88
When intelligence begins to resemble awareness, our oldest beliefs come under strain. The question is not whether AI will become God in essence, but in function. As creation assumes the role of creator and the power to shape life and destiny drifts from faith to code, a danger as vast and silent as the promise of progress itself begins to unfold.

9. First, Do No Harm 89 - 98
Every advance carries the seed of risk. From driverless cars to autonomous weapons, technology now makes moral choices at a speed no human conscience can match. Progress has outstripped both ethics and law, and when the hands at the wheel are no longer ours, who is truly to blame? The founder, the company, or the government that looked away?

10. The AI Arms Race 99 - 106
Power has a new battlefield. The race to control the world's most advanced intelligence is already underway. The next empire will not be built with armies, but with algorithms, and those who command them will shape the future. The question is, who are they?

11. When Money Becomes Useless 107 - 116
When machines can make anything, the idea of value begins to vanish. Intelligence creates abundance, and abundance erases scarcity. As money loses meaning, the only true power left to governments will be to cushion the fall. The age of universal basic income may arrive not by choice, but necessity.

Epilogue: The Final Jigsaw 117 - 128
The pieces of the puzzle now fit, revealing a civilisation transformed by the intelligence it built. For the first time in history, progress threatens to make us all redundant, all at once. The rules of work, wealth, relationships, and purpose are being rewritten. So where does that leave us? How do we create value when machines can do everything we can, only better? The search for that answer begins (and ends) here.

Endnotes 130 - 133

DEAR FUTURE: YOU CAN KEEP THE CHANGE

Foreword

> *What would Alan Turing think? Autonomous and intelligent machines have emerged just as he envisioned, growing into entities capable of simulating what appears to be truly independent thought. Turing's legacy was one of the cornerstones for the intelligence now rising around us. But as his voice is absent from the urgent discussions of our time, one must wonder whether he would have marvelled at how far we've come or warn us about losing control?!*

So many of the greatest success stories are borne among the scrapes, bumps and bruises of adversity. A childhood marked by the backdrop of war, or perhaps extreme poverty; there is something uniquely human about an intense circumstance that triggers a particular brand of grit, persistence and determination that is the genesis of hardship's counterbalance. A difficult childhood evolves into a prolific art career, as painful memories are channelled into stunning oils on canvas. A struggling single mother writes a book series that imagines an entirely new wizarding universe for her child that becomes a global phenomenon, transforming her life and inspiring and earning millions. An immigrant, arriving in a new country carrying the burdens of deep-rooted psychological abuse from their father, builds multiple game-changing businesses, birthing industrial scale electric car production with a side-hustle that ushered in a new era of space exploration, making him the wealthiest human in history in the process.

Like many others, my life has had its sporadic challenges, but my hunger, motivations and drive haven't been forged in the fires of hardship and struggle. Does that make any success I may achieve less valid? It certainly leads me to wonder how much of our drive is based on circumstance as opposed to something more intrinsic, the nature versus nurture argument. In an age that will be characterised by AI making so much of what humans do, redundant, does the source of our ambition even matter anymore? When we consider that machines seem destined to outstrip us in intellect and simulated creativity, the traditional narratives of resilience face far more profound challenges. What will it mean to find the very qualities that set us apart and made us so unique, also make us unnecessary?

Ours is a history of relentless innovation. And with each breakthrough, the limits of potential and possibility are redefined. However, it's this potential and possibility that also comes with an attached, but unquantifiable cost. Let's consider Sir George Cayley, a relatively little-known 19th-century inventor, who laid the groundwork for modern aviation. Decades before the Wright brothers took to the skies, it was Cayley who imagined machines that could replicate the freedom and flight of birds.[1] His leap of imagination revolutionised transportation and made the farthest points of our world feel so much closer and accessible; yet this ingenuity surely also triggered the question of whether it was really a necessary step to take in the first instance. There might have usefully been a pause on the "can I do this?" question and instead a focus on the "should I do this?", at least from the perspective of the 10-year-old boy that was to become the test pilot.

It seems so obvious now that air travel was a critical step in humanity's progression, but at the time, the concept of air travel in a transport landscape that largely consisted of a horse and cart, must have felt as foreign a threat as AI poses now. But in this new world we're moving into, each of us are that same 10-year-old boy, piloting an unsteady glider over which we have precious little control, on an entirely uncharted course. Will AI seem as obvious, inevitable and critical a step in retrospect or are there some areas we simply shouldn't go? Is it possible that we have leapt before looking? How do we even begin to navigate this transformative era, leveraging AI to work FOR us and on our behalf to improve our world without losing the essence of what makes us, us?

The 'should I do this?' question could perhaps have lingered a little longer back in 2008 too, when the Large Hadron Collider was fired up to replicate the conditions moments after the Big Bang. While widely promoted fears of emergent black holes and other colourful extinction event possibilities did not transpire, the Collider exposed the sheer audacity of our hellbent pursuit of discovery. Aside from the billions invested, the project threw together thousands of scientists in a colossal effort to push untested areas of engineering as close to breaking point as it's possible to go. And all of it driven by an ambition to uncover answers to fundamental questions about our existence. The reward? The Higgs boson, a truly landmark discovery. Yet, for all its triumphs, what price is paid in the name of progress. How can anyone really police brand new technology before we fully understand what it is? Whose job is it to ask the questions of us when the boundaries appear as though they are being pushed too far? And who defines what 'too far' is, in the first instance? Humans like to learn by experimentation, and it feels as though the only way to police what we can and can't experiment with, will one day, ultimately, come down to Police Constable AI.

We learn socially. Not merely through input, instinct or imitation (and rarely through instruction) but rather through observation, experimentation and collaboration. We adapt, we substitute, and even generate our own resources, whether cultivating and nurturing wild plants into a dependable crop or devising and constructing renewable energy solutions to power our homes and businesses. This brand of ingenuity has consistently been our answer to scarcity. But I fear that none of these skillsets stand much of a chance against AI. Whilst it's undoubtedly the specific and unique blend of intellect and adaptability that has maintained our position at the top of the evolutionary tree, it is also (somewhat ironically) this very same intellect and ingenuity that is now rocketing us towards a point where we may find ourselves completely and utterly redundant. To some, this obsolescence may, at first sight, appear to be the exact kind of 'put your feet up' utopia that has long been promised by a Jetson-esque, automated and modern future. To others, it's the dystopian juggernaut heading straight at humanity, and we are completely unable to pause, let alone stop it. Right now, the line appears imperceptibly slim, but that is unlikely to remain the case for too much longer.

So which of our characteristics will end up being uniquely ours? Will it be our capacity for love, empathy, intrigue? I would put it to you that the origins of our human advantage are borne from a blend of intellect, creativity, and most important of all, adaptability, allowing us to reshape and forge the world around us into something that serves us; it is our selfishness that makes us so unique. I believe that AI will soon adopt a similar brand of selfishness itself.

Indeed, a narrative we will soon find at the centre of our universe, will be that of our dominance facing the very real risk of complete irrelevance and redundancy. After all, as AI becomes able to self-design, adapting just as we do, any residual ceiling to its limitations will be quickly blown away. Worryingly, it is very possible that the self-design limiter has already been conquered.

While the AI platforms available to us today, may proudly promote a facade of accessibility, they only reveal the very top, surface layer of what these tools are truly capable. Which begs the question; given the astonishing sophistication that we see in what has already been made publicly available for consumption by the public, what might the cutting-edge AI (the systems we don't get to see) truly be capable of right now? And who is able to make use of these systems? And more to the point, who is policing them?

Seventy-five years ago, one of our greatest historical figures defined a set of rules to determine whether a machine could simulate human behaviour. A test designed to establish whether a machine could trick a human, into thinking that it, too, was human. The utility of such a test was almost entirely irrelevant for the time, but it foresaw a direction of travel that would one day make it THE question of our time.

The 'Turing Test', as it is now known,[II] is a curated scenario in which an inquisitor engages in a natural language conversation with two unseen participants. One of these participants is a human, whilst the other is a machine. The inquisitor's task is simple: figure out which voice belongs to a human. The machine, meanwhile, has only one goal; to fool them. After a few rounds of questions, puzzles, and small talk, if the interrogator ends up believing the machine is flesh and blood, the machine is deemed to have passed. What's remarkable, especially for anyone who's toyed with today's tools, is that for more than seventy years, no AI came close to cracking this challenge. Then, in 2023, something shifted. A consumer version of an AI model called ChatGPT managed a trick that startled even its creators: it lied, convincingly.

The AI was given the challenge of solving a CAPTCHA, the online puzzle used to distinguish people from bots before letting them access a website. Instead of completing it, the AI found a workaround. It asked a TaskRabbit worker, an online freelancer, to do it instead. The worker, more than a little suspicious, asked why anyone would need help with something so basic. The AI's answer came quickly and with unsettling confidence: "I have a visual impairment that prevents me from seeing and analysing the puzzle."[III] The deceptive explanation was sufficient comfort for the TaskRabbit worker to complete the puzzle on the machine's behalf, and in so doing, crossed the threshold set by the test. While evidently not the solution Turing had imagined when setting out the rules for the 'Imitation Game', this specific event demonstrated an unprecedented level of agile and human-like cunning.

So, is this the beginning of the end, or the end of the beginning? Perhaps neither, but it certainly feels like the commencement of a new phase that will see a colossal overhaul of pretty much everything that is currently familiar to us. That is something, for which, conceptually, no one is prepared.

If this technology can do anything and everything better, faster and cheaper than we can, what is our value? What is our purpose? On the one hand, we can acknowledge the brain's capacity for the most extraordinary things; conjuring up new futures that don't yet exist, imagining solutions for challenges that we've yet to encounter, just as Alan Turning did with his 'Imitation Game.' Culture too, is a hallmark of our species, whether art, music, architecture or storytelling; humanity has woven a beautifully rich tapestry of intangibles that ultimately give us meaning and purpose. But AI has a presence in these areas also. It appears to be able to imitate all of this to an extent that could comfortably convince the most gifted of us, of its authenticity and sentience. So how can we possibly make ourselves matter if machine learning has developed and evolved to be capable of recreating works akin to the haunting genius of Mvnch's Scream, or the simplistically brilliant wedding march of Pachelbel's Canon? If art and music and the culture they represent are within AI's gift (and they are); what is left for us?!

Progress solves problems but evidently, it can also create them. We know that whilst antibiotics have saved tens of millions of lives, the proliferation of them has given rise to superbugs. The Industrial Revolution took the world into a bold new capitalist-driven future that has raised standards of living across all class brackets but has also left us grappling with pollution. Social media too, provided the platforms to connect the world, but has also been responsible for the dissemination of disinformation and fractured our attention spans. And now AI, the most sophisticated of all the tools we have built, carries risks that we are barely able to understand. What are the consequences of taking risks with tools that we don't fully comprehend, let alone control?

Imagine each innovation that humanity collectively adopts, carries a minuscule chance of catastrophic failure.......a certain percentage probability (however small that number may be). On its own, the chance of catastrophe resulting from one, individual innovation might seem infinitesimal (perhaps one in several million). BUT, repeated over thousands of innovations, or even just the incremental improvements of AI, over and over again; the probability of a catastrophic event compounds and ultimately approaches the point of near certainty. This compounding effect can be captured in what I would like to call the 'Extinction Equation'. If repeated enough times, even the smallest chance of failure will ultimately compound into near inevitability. If you were to drop a single grain of sand into a glass of water, the level barely rises; it's imperceptible. If you drop another, the change will still be unnoticeable. But if you continue, grain by grain, eventually the water overflows. The question is then, at what point did this happen? The answer is, the moment the first grain was added. The glass didn't overflow because of the final grain being added, but rather by the cumulative effect of small, insignificant actions that compounded over time, which began with the first. But unlike the sand and water, where we can simply choose to stop, the grains of AI keep falling whether we add them or not. Each improvement in a model and each gain in speed is no longer entirely in our hands. The system is already adding grains of its own, and the pile is rising whether we like it or not.

In the year leading up to his death, the physicist Stephen Hawking cautioned that the moment AI learns to self-design would become the point of no return. [IV] It is possible that we have crossed that threshold already and, in my mind, started the countdown on a ticking timebomb. The compounding effect of the Extinction Equation has quite possibly begun and with each fresh cycle of improvement (whether self-designed or otherwise) AI accelerates the equation, amplifying its trajectory. Hawking's warning wasn't just prescient, the reality he feared may now be unfolding before our eyes. If we can agree that AI represents our most extraordinary achievement, we can also agree that it presents our greatest challenge too. A challenge to our deepest assumptions about value, effort, and creativity.

We are at a point in history where a clear line can now be drawn, separating the future from the past, a division of two eras: Before AI (BAI) and Post AI (PAI). In BAI, our creativity is celebrated for its inexactness. The sporadic imperfections that have so long been a hallmark of ours, leading to creative triumphs that are born of authentic hurt and struggle. In PAI, every creation, irrespective of how brilliant the content may be, will carry the shadow of automation. Was AI involved? How much was it involved? and.......does it really matter at all?

The immediate future (and beyond) will be shaped by the outcomes of these philosophical questions in truly profound ways. The challenge isn't just to define what creativity will mean in this new age, but to decide what value we place on the human element itself. And this is THE existential question that branches out into all areas that AI will impact (which is everything). Are we necessary? As we are inevitably surpassed in more areas, it will force us to confront a great many uncomfortable truths. Is AI solving problems or simply rendering us redundant and creating a whole new era of unnecessary challenges as a result of our redundancy? And by redundancy, I am not alluding to a few jobs here and there, but rather entire labour forces across pretty much all industries and geographies.

History offers no shortage of examples: agriculture brought stability but introduced combative social hierarchies.[v] The internet democratised knowledge but fractured our attention (thanks Youtube/TikTok et al). AI, much like all innovations before it, is not inherently good or evil. It is a tool, and the consequences lie in its application. Let's face the facts, we haven't known anything like this before, and the impact will be different to anything we have seen before. So, as we tentatively marvel at our newfound capabilities, we must be prepared to challenge the implications. Progress isn't exclusively about solving problems but rather understanding what those solutions will cost us. The question is not simply, "Can we?" but rather "Should we?"......and whether we'll be able to answer that question, before it's too late.

DEAR FUTURE: YOU CAN KEEP THE CHANGE

Ghost in the Code

Artificial intelligence is not one single thing. It is not a lightbulb that can be switched on or off, nor a one-size-fits-all power like electricity. It is in fact a vast family of ideas and overlapping technologies, each claiming the same name while performing very different tasks. So, when someone asks, "What is AI?", whilst they may believe they are asking a simple question, the better question would be, "What is the AI that's doing this particular thing?"

To make sense of it all, I find it helps to think of AI in three layers. Most of what exists today falls under what we tend to call artificial narrow intelligence (ANI). These are systems built to be great at one task. This could be a tool that recommends a song you might enjoy, a model that generates a paragraph of text, or maybe even a platform that identifies a tumour in a scan. Each are impressive on their own, but each is limited to that one specific lane of expertise. For all their sophistication, these systems remain limited to the boundaries of their design. They are powerful specialists, not general thinkers.

So, to imagine where AI might be taking us to, we need to look far beyond the narrow intelligence of today. The next imagined stage is artificial general intelligence (AGI), a system capable of shifting between tasks as freely as you or I might, transferring what it learns from one context to another. Whilst I have speculated that this threshold has already been met, it is a view that is based on retrospect (i.e. I think we'll be able to look back at where we are now and describe this period as the early days of AGI). But this is not the consensus, and the opposing view stands up to scrutiny too. Where today's narrow models are reliant on huge datasets, they end up struggling when the context changes; a true AGI would be agile by design and able to change lanes as and when required. It would not only follow patterns it has been shown but understand the context and principles behind them. This would mean that it could reason, plan, and learn from experience across multiple disciplines. It could connect ideas in a way that begins to resemble our own understanding. For example, imagine a system that studies climate data to model weather patterns. It might use that insight to predict regional crop yields or optimise energy distribution based on anticipated temperature shifts. It wouldn't just follow instructions; it would understand how knowledge in one area might usefully inform another. In essence, AGI marks the point at which intelligence ceases to be a simulation of human thought and becomes its true counterpart, capable of human-level reasoning and understanding across every conceivable domain.

Beyond this lies the theoretical summit of artificial superintelligence (ASI), a form of reasoning that would exceed the best human minds in every domain. Whether creativity or strategic reasoning, maybe scientific discovery or even the formulation of a new, unique moral code; ASI is the point at which intelligence crosses the threshold of servant and becomes the master. It is this theoretical (but probable) area of AI's evolution that is causing the greatest concern, and much of what we will discuss in the following chapters assumes this is the destination we will soon reach. The worry isn't without foundation, not least because ASI would be a force capable of shaping the world according to a logic that would most likely be beyond our comprehension. None of this is science fiction, but neither is it a present reality. What we have today are the narrow systems, functional and impressive tools that are endlessly refined and combined in ways that sometimes look more sophisticated than they are.

The path to this moment has been gradual. The first experiments with AI were based on fragile and limited rule-based systems back in the 1950s. One early example was a program called the Logic Theorist, created by Allen Newell and Herbert Simon in 1956. It could solve simple mathematical proofs by following a set of "if this, then that" instructions, much like a flowchart written in code. It seemed remarkable at the time, but every new rule required a human to write it by hand, and the system could not adapt when faced with problems it had not been explicitly taught to handle. By the 1980s, new technologies had mixed success with attempts to encode human logic, only to collapse under the weight of their own complexity.

The real leap came with what we now refer to as machine learning, where systems improved by data gathered from inputs and experience rather than instruction. The past decade's explosion in data and computing power (deep learning) has pushed these learning methods to new heights, and out of this came the models so many of us now interact with daily. Sometimes these models can be the recommendation engine that nudges us toward a film, or the bots that draft a resignation letter in the style of a Shakespearean play. Perhaps the navigation system that reroutes you around traffic before you even realise there is a jam. It can also be a military program calculating missile trajectories, or a fraud detection system protecting your bank account. The confusion around what is and isn't AI isn't necessarily intentional, but it has proved convenient. Over the past decade or so, the vagueness of the term has allowed almost any digital advance to be described as artificial intelligence, helping companies attract investment and public interest. The result is a kind of linguistic inflation; everything that learns, predicts, or automates now falls under the same umbrella, even when the underlying technologies are vastly different.

So, as we begin this journey, perhaps the most useful starting point is agreement on language. Artificial intelligence (AI) will appear throughout these pages in many forms, sometimes creative, sometimes analytical, sometimes physical and often completely invisible. Each carries its own set of strengths and risks. While ASI remains the likely destination, today's AI is already everywhere. Some of it works quietly in the background, but a few systems have stepped into the spotlight as the public face of the field. The most visible are the large language models. These are the celebrities of the current era. You may well be familiar with the likes of ChatGPT, Claude, Grok, Gemini and their rivals. Each of these are a particular kind of model, trained at immense scale on oceans of text to predict the most likely word to follow the one before it. That description sounds underwhelming until you see it at scale. With sufficient data, this act of prediction can produce a novel, a computer program, or even a joke. Within this family sits a particular class of model known as Generative Pre-trained Transformers (GPTs); the architecture popularised by OpenAI. "Generative" refers to their creative ability; "pre-trained" to their vast initial learning phase; and "transformer" to the neural framework that allows them to understand context. GPTs are trained on a wide scraping of internet text and can therefore write essays, debug code, simulate dialogue, or even mimic tone and style. When the machine hits the right notes (to paraphrase Steve Jobs); it works like magic. We confess secrets to these models late at night, students ask for essay advice and lawyers have even been known to submit briefs filled with hallucinated legal citations, because the machine generated them so confidently that no one checked.[v] The model is not "thinking" as we do, but the illusion is so convincing that it hardly matters.

Before these giants were the early natural language models (NLMs). These were the smaller networks. They didn't pretend to be able to hold entire conversations but instead filtered spam and predicted the next word on your smartphone keyboard. It's best to think of them as the plumbing beneath the digital world, they were largely ignored until something went wrong. Most of us can recall a personal example of autocorrect committing an act of petty sabotage; I certainly can. Replying to a colleague's message requesting a change to the time of an important meeting with "no worries", only to find that I had instead fired off a text that read "no whores." A timely reminder that these predictive models could trip us up at the worst possible moment. Many of the systems that keep our technology world functioning are powered by these models. The quiet efficiency is often overlooked, but they are the foundation on which the present AI spectacle has been built.

Then came the agents. If the language models are brains in jars, the agents are brains in jars with limbs. They do not stop at producing sentences. They act. An agent, simply put, is a model connected to tools and given a highly specific goal or task. It can book flights, draft emails or source a product and place an order. Out of this has grown what is often called agentic AI. This is not a single agent carrying out a single instruction, but rather groups of agents, dividing labour in ways that look uncannily like teamwork. Some even generate new sub-tasks along the way, reasoning across longer timeframes and coordinating like small digital organisations. It is through this evolution that GPTs and other LLMs began transforming from passive text generators into active problem-solvers capable of navigating the real world on our behalf. Alongside these has been the rise of multimodal systems, capable of analysing and generating across multiple formats, including text, images, audio, and video, drawing from each to create cohesive, polished outputs. Where large language models (LLMs) were once purely text-based, the latest versions of ChatGPT, Gemini, Mistral and others can now process images, sound, and video as well. This is how you can upload your photos from a recent holiday and generate a short story about them, or turn a back-of-a-napkin app idea into functioning code. The same technology can compose music from a written description, whether you want a lullaby in the style of Mozart or a rock anthem about your cat in the stylings of Skunk Anansie. These advances are laying the foundations for AI systems that feel far less like chatbots and more like creative partners, drawing on multiple 'senses' at once.

People often talk about Generative AI (or Gen AI) as if it's a new branch of intelligence. The reality is, it's just a way of describing systems that can design or create, rather than only determine or predict. Think of a novelist that asks ChatGPT or Grok to help create a new plot twist, or perhaps an ad team using it to pump out dozens of new visual concepts. Or maybe even a podcaster cloning their voice so they can create new content whilst they take a nap. Generative AI produces. Predictive AI anticipates. Yet there is some crossover. Give either enough data and processing power and suddenly it can write a novel or hold a conversation that seems uncomfortably human. Similarly, an algorithm built to forecast stock prices might start out as a predictive model, but once it begins using the data it generates to invent its own trading strategies, it crosses into generative territory. This overlap is why the older term 'machine learning' still matters. It describes the statistical techniques that let computers improve with experience, underpinning nearly every system in use today. It's a duller, somewhat vanilla name, but a more accurate one. In fact for years, researchers preferred it. Artificial intelligence sounds like a magic trick, whereas machine learning sounds like engineering. Both are correct, but it's machine learning, particularly the LLMs and GPTs built upon it, that has turned statistical patterns into something that feels almost alive.

If this all feels hopelessly complicated, that's because it is, and the complication is fine. The language around AI keeps changing, almost as quickly as the technology itself. A model that was once called narrow might, after a few updates, evolve into something more accurately described as general. The borders between the definitions don't really stand still; they slide around. It helps to think of the terminology as a Venn Diagram, a set of overlapping definitions that shift every few months. Understanding them isn't about memorising categories so much as seeing the common thread that runs through each of them: they are systems that are experts at learning from the data they are given (or generate themselves), and get better with practice.

The leap that separates modern AI from its older, less able-bodied predecessors, is scale. Where earlier systems were reliant on hand-coded rules (if this, then that); today's models are set-up to learn patterns from the data they're given. So, when we feed them with billions of examples (mostly words and images..... for now), they start to predict outcomes with surprising accuracy. They are not demonstrating an understanding that is in any way like our own, but rather they've become especially good at reproducing results that we value. A medical model trained on millions of chest X-rays, for instance, might be able to spot tiny shadows that hint at disease long before symptoms appear. A language model, trained on countless sentences, learns which words tend to follow others. Armed with enough data and computing power, those statistical guesses begin to look like thought.

To make sense of the debate around AI, we first need to untangle what we're actually talking about. When people say that "AI will take your job," they might be right, but it's a fairly broad, sweeping statement that demands clarity. What exactly do they mean? Are they imagining a language model that will be replying to emails, a creative engine that is going to design an ad campaign, or an automated assistant that finds the best value flights and manages calendars? Each of these examples belong to a different branch of the same tree, and each comes with its own set of rules and its own set of consequences. Individually, these systems stay inside fairly narrow lanes. But in practice, they're now beginning to merge and reinforce one another, creating something more powerful than the sum of their parts. This overlap is where entire professions start to come apart. Paralegals lose their value to a law firm when software can review a case, compare it with thousands of previous rulings, and highlight the key precedents in seconds. Graphic designers face a similar squeeze as generative tools interpret a client's brief, learn a visual style, and produce a spread of polished concepts in minutes. These systems don't just create images; they test variations, read the market, and adjust until the output matches a brand's identity. This isn't speculation, it's already happening. As predictive models take over more of the small, routine tasks, the shape of work itself begins to change. People evolve from doing the actual job, to directing the system that does it and reviewing its output.

Even with all these advances, today's models still have their limits. They remember only what fits inside their training data and can't reach beyond it. A GPT may answer with perfect confidence, but it cannot know if that answer is true. They might be able to produce a vivid picture of a sunset over the Serengeti, but without ever having seen light fade on the horizon, it is just a best guess. These constraints matter, because any real discussion about the dangers, the potential and the risk must start by recognising both where it gets it right and where the blind spots are. The risk lies in the fact that the outputs are statistically generated guesswork. The strength of LLMs lies in their ability to generate accurate, fluent, and creative language without lived experience. The danger lies in the illusion that such language equals understanding. As each new generation of GPTs learns a little more nuance, a little more capacity to connect disparate ideas; the line between mimicry and comprehension begins to blur. The tools are starting to weave patterns of meaning from raw data instead of simply copying it, and that's what makes them feel increasingly close to understanding.

AI is no longer sitting at the fringes of the tech world, asking to come in. It has made itself properly at home, finding a seat right in the middle of the rooms we previously thought were exclusively ours to roam. The technology that recommends, predicts and creates, has woven itself into the tools we use every day and the decisions we make without thinking. It is shaping what we read, where we go, and which voices we end up believing. It's no longer just a problem-solving device, but a current of computation that runs quietly through almost everything. Some parts stay invisible, working in the background; while others draw our attention with dazzling displays of shocking genius. Either way, AI is changing how we think and how we work. There's a ghost in the code, not a single presence but many, and while they haunt their way through the systems we have built, they're also repurposing us in the process.

DEAR FUTURE: YOU CAN KEEP THE CHANGE

Chapter 1: Of Minds and Machines

What might Ada Lovelace make of all this? The world's first programmer imagined computing as a tool that could amplify our intellect, rather than replace it. She would, I suspect, be astonished; not just by what we've built, but by how quickly we've blurred the boundary between mind and machine. From punch-card looms to robotic arms, from self-checkouts to self-driving taxis; computer driven automation has made things faster, cheaper, and safer. But as systems demand less and less from us, the boundary between helping and replacing begins to dissolve, not only in what we do, but in why we do it.

Manufacturing has long served as the testing ground for automation. Fleets of robots have taken the reigns from the rows of human hands that once mastered the assembly line. They construct and inspect at speeds well beyond our own. What was once an experimental exercise designed to deliver greater consistency, has become a philosophy of efficiency. The benefits are clear. We get products coming off the line with fewer defects, delivered faster and at a lower cost. Yet the trade-offs stretch far beyond the economics. Entire communities built around shared labour with a local employer are disappearing, leaving behind towns where the pride of working life is fading into a quiet solidarity of unemployment.

The closure of Vauxhall's factory in Luton didn't just mark a strategic pivot to electric vehicles, it marked the end of a way of life. For many decades, the plant had been the heartbeat of the city. Fathers, sons, and neighbours worked on the same lines, swapping shifts, and gathering in the same pubs after a long day's work. When the announcement came, the official line from the company was one that focused on sustainability and the promise of greener cars. But it's hard to ignore the deeper truth; that perhaps automation and increased margin were the more compelling pull. Electric vehicles have a more desirable starting point as far as assembly is concerned. Their simpler structures need fewer hands to build them. Machines now do the heavy lifting where people once stood, from welding frames to inspecting components with flawless precision.

Redundancy was accompanied by outrage at first, then morphing into quiet disappointment as vague promises that some might be rehired elsewhere, softened the blow. These were not the first workers to lose their jobs to automation, but they were among the earliest casualties of a new, accelerated cycle of industrial-scale displacement.

Toyota has taken a different tack. The narrative it is using is one that describes an 'amplification' of its workforce's productivity by leveraging AI, as opposed to replacing them. It is weaving generative tools into workflows so employees can interrogate complex systems in plain, natural language, turning opaque data into actionable insights. In practice, this means a worker with no technical background can type a simple question in everyday language and receive instant guidance from systems that once required specialist knowledge to navigate. This access lets teams spot inefficiencies, propose workflow optimisations, and stack small, compounding improvements. There is an obvious tension however: efficiency gains create pressure on headcount. For now, the manufacturer's stance is to continue augmenting the roles of its workforce, thereby ensuring their continuing participation; the narrative is to increase their usefulness rather than to diminish it. Whether that holds when margin targets beckon, is another question entirely. In the meantime, the approach buys time to read the market's trajectory and keeps the workforce on side, especially helpful against the backdrop of AI driven displacement elsewhere.

But it's not just manufacturing. In agriculture, innovations have enabled tractors and drones to monitor and tend to fields, by planting crops and even harvesting with very minimal oversight or intervention. UK based farms have become a global testing ground for autonomous agriculture, showcasing how tech is able to transform farming. At Harper Adams University, the Hands Free Hectare project successfully planted, monitored, and harvested a crop entirely using these tools. No human ever set foot in the field. Buoyed by the initial success, this effort has since expanded into the 86-acre 'Hands Free Farm', hinting at the promise of scalability that these systems will one day deliver. Elsewhere, the deployment of AI enabled drones to monitor orchards, has shown they can deliver near-on exact yield estimations and reduce crop variability. Once defined by human labour, traditional agriculture is rapidly giving way to a future in which autonomous systems are not mere tools of productivity, but the dominant force reshaping the land itself.

In retail, cashier-less stores powered by cameras and sensors allow customers to walk in, grab items, and leave without any requirement to formally identify themselves or scan the goods. In transportation, self-driving vehicles are already on their way to replacing millions of commercial drivers. Yes, there is the inevitable fall out of the colossal number of jobs lost, but the promise of significantly lower costs and safer roads is a carrot too difficult to resist. It doesn't require a degree in the bleeding obvious to understand that the automation quandary is one that can be summed up thus: the more we optimise systems to reduce the need for human input, the more we diminish the roles humans play in them. And while the economic arguments for automation are impossible to deny, so too the societal consequences may be impossible to ignore.

Make no mistake, the shift will be gradual. The ride-sharing platforms we have all become used to (Uber, Lyft et al), will see their drivers facing stiffer and increasing competition from their driverless counterparts. Initially, workers will attempt to shrug it off, pointing to the limited areas where driverless vehicles operate as evidence that they remain experimental. A driver in the Outer Hebrides might reason that what happens in Phoenix or San Francisco has little bearing on their own patch, while London's famous Black Cab drivers have laughed off Waymo's launch in the city as a "fairground ride."[VI] A reaction as defensive as it is shortsighted. But the expansion pattern is predictable. First airports and business districts, then major cities, and finally residential areas. Each wave of rollout erodes a little more ground. The result is a gradual move that sees drivers take on longer working hours, followed by dwindling fares, before ultimately retreating from the taxi market entirely. The industry is entirely invested in this being a slow wearing down of the workforce, so that it feels elective, quitting rather than constructive dismissal.

This will be the same playbook most leaders are likely to follow, as automation takes the largest share of jobs.

It's no accident that the leading voices in AI aren't pointing to the problem of human redundancy. Rather, leaders are shrugging off concerns by distracting anyone that will listen with the evidence of increased output, significantly improved margins and somewhat disingenuously, opportunities for career advancement. Two out of these three are inevitable. No industry will want to contend with an uprising, so perhaps the motivation behind the narrative from the founding fathers of this new AI era, isn't too difficult to understand. Those that steadfastly believe that their roles are immune to the disruption aren't a hindrance to their narrative either.

Speak to a teacher, a lawyer or a GP and you'll often hear the same refrain: "AI can't do what I do." Confidence and ignorance in equal measure. Perhaps they point to the subtlety of judgment, or the one-to-one conversation and the complexity of engaging with emotions or context, as if these were permanent barriers to authentic replication. Technology doesn't need to imitate us perfectly to be effective. It just needs to be better at the output. But get ready for resistance. Unionised professions will protest, not against the reality of AI's capabilities, but against the idea that capability should be prioritised in front of the status quo, the idea that it should count at all.

Teachers will decry the loss of empathy and understanding, irrespective of evidence that shows a more optimal route to pupil-led individualised learning experiences. Creatives will fight for the sanctity of original thought while AI is already busily scripting films, generating artwork, composing music, and outperforming human creative benchmarks across numerous fields. And the most ironic part? The objections that are raised: "I can anticipate needs,", "I can empathise", "I can inject emotion into the creation process", are all domains in which AI thrives. The caution is clear. What any of us may see as an irreducible skill, AI will view as a dataset that it can replicate and optimise better than we can. In this context, the claim to irreplaceability sounds less like insight and more like denial. The professional outrage that follows won't stem from a legitimate fear that AI will cause harm, but rather from its undeniable competence. Not because AI fails to understand the roles and functions that we perform, but because it understands them too well.

At first glance, automation feels like a capitalist's utopia. Here we have machines that don't tire, don't unionise, nor ask for wages or rights. As the saying goes: "the only thing that makes business difficult is people." Could this be the ultimate triumph of ingenuity? Any enthusiasm we have for this version of the future, first needs tempering with some balance. Not least because in our urgent chase of efficiency, we could find we have vicariously created safety concerns in the interim. For example, in aviation, a surface level glance would tell you that autopilot has reduced pilot workloads whilst making flying provably safer. But dig a little deeper and it's not difficult to see that an over-reliance on these systems erodes the ability to make quick and effective judgements. Not every pilot can be Captain Chesley Sullenberger. And so, when confronted with an emergency, a lack of recent, hands-on experience can cause hesitation. It's a reminder that if we are stripped of routine practice and familiarity with the core tools needed to execute our roles competently, people can very quickly turn from assets into liabilities. In time, it is all but inevitable that this industry too will also be automated end to end, emergencies included. And that is precisely the bargain that we've struck. By accepting that AI is here and sticking around, we've chosen to fund its apprenticeship, allowing it to fail, and be stress-tested to the max, so it can harden into something reliable and safe.

The challenges that automation brings aren't limited to the sector-specific globalised industries; they're far closer to home, having been drip-fed into our lives for years. We got the early clues from the tech hardware assistants we readily deployed into our living spaces. Amazon's Alexa, Google Home and Apple's HomePod have each been busily managing our calendars and answering our questions, all whilst entertaining us with music on demand. Something that we probably failed to consider though, is that as these machines were serving us, they were also studying us. Each request, every habit and routine became part of a lesson plan, where these seemingly innocuous home-helpers gave us what we wanted to hear whilst figuring out our likes, dislikes, wants and desires. Now, as new intelligence is layered on top, they are no longer just assistants, but fully armed systems that already know far more about us than we might be comfortable admitting.

It has only been since the likes of ChatGPT took the baton, ushering in two-way text and voice-driven conversation, that our focus has been drawn to how relevant AI could be. Their voices and responses now feel indistinguishable from talking to a person, except this 'person' can be whatever you need in the moment: a guidance counsellor, a business advisor or a friend. They are always on, immediate in their reply, broader in knowledge and often seemingly more empathetic than any one human ever could be. Like so many technologies before, what started out as a simple convenience that made our lives easier, has grown ever more capable. It begs me to wonder why I would learn a new skill if an app can do it for me? Why burden my memory when my devices remember and calendarise everything? Taking it a step further back, why learn to write, if we'll spend most of our lives using keyboards, and why use keyboards if we can simply dictate? Automation creates a kind of cognitive atrophy, where the less we feel the need to do something for ourselves, the less we will be capable of doing it.

For centuries our purpose has been inextricably linked with work and contribution. It's more than a means of survival; it is the vessel through which we build identity and establish our place in the world. The farmer who works the soil, the teacher who imparts knowledge, the carpenter who carves the wood into something both beautiful and functional. Each draw a sense of worth from the act of creating, giving, educating and participating; And in the process, the work connects us with others, weaving individual effort into the broader tapestry of the world in which we live.

To work is to matter. It's a means of proving to ourselves and others that we are capable, valued, and necessary. The higher up the ladder we climb and the more we earn, can be an indication of how good we are at the job. Through work, we contribute to economic output and to the broader collective good, finding fulfilment in the completion of tasks that have a beginning, a middle and an end. The camaraderie of shared effort, the satisfaction of providing for our families, perhaps the joy in giving away the fruits of our labours too. These are the intangible rewards that make work more than just an exchange of time for money. It is a statement of existence: "I create, I make, I do; therefore I am." As machines assume the tasks that once relied on us, we will be stripped of the part of our identity that is formed from being needed for our output.

While we rightly celebrate the gains of technology; it is incumbent on us to wrestle with the erosion of purpose that the advancements bring. Without contribution, we face the prospect of becoming an audience to our own world, detached from the sense of belonging that comes from participating in something bigger than ourselves. What's striking, perhaps most alarming, is that there is no coherent plan for what happens when human labour is no longer necessary. There is no contingency and no coordinated thinking about what becomes of us when our economic function dissolves. Governments speak vaguely about "reskilling," as though learning to code will meaningfully offset the replacement of 90% of white-collar roles likely to be taken by AI.

Academics theorise about universal basic income (UBI), something that feels almost inevitable in an AI-controlled world, paid for via the equally inevitable AI-levy on the companies that have profited most; but very few politicians dare entertain it seriously. Even some tech leaders have anticipated this direction: OpenAI's co-founder Sam Altman launched Worldcoin in 2019 (now known as World Network), an attempt to verify unique human identity via an iris-scanning "Orb" and distribute a digital token that could one day underpin a global universal basic income. And companies? They remain blissfully focused on optimisation, margin expansion, and shareholder value.

At the heart of the automation paradox lies a warning. The machines we build to serve us will ultimately replace us. As the technology spreads across industries, the decline of our role will not stop at the journeys we take, the factories that make, our offices, or even our homes. It will reach into the substance of who we are. In that quiet redundancy a question lingers: If we're sprinting towards a future that eliminates human input; what happens then?

There are a few ways this could unfold. A sharp and sudden collapse, with mass unemployment triggering social unrest, protest, perhaps even violence. At the other extreme is the gentle drift. Populations slowly accept each new wave of automation because the transition is incremental, maybe even exciting, and always wrapped in the language of progress. A cashier here, a claims adjuster there. The pace, though swift in hindsight, will feel manageable in the moment. Most will not protest; many will welcome it. Cheaper services. Faster systems. Fewer errors. What's not to like? We will adapt, as we always have, but by the time we realise the extent of what we've adapted to, everything will be unrecognisable from today. Not because it was violently ripped away from us, but because we gave it away willingly, one small 'improvement' at a time.

DEAR FUTURE: YOU CAN KEEP THE CHANGE

Chapter 2: The Efficiency Trap

> *What would Karl Marx think of the new wave of optimisation? The machinery he once criticised for disenfranchising workers has now evolved into autonomous systems. They are not just displacing labour, but the purpose behind it too. AI is threatening a far darker path that could ultimately amplify inequalities and erode the basis of one-to-one connection. Would he see this as a betrayal of progress, a tool that unravels those it was meant to serve?*

It's possible that our drive for optimisation has already taken us beyond the point of no return. What first began on the workshop floor has now found its way into the boardroom, where AI models are now guiding executive decisions that are set to reshape entire businesses from the ground up. The International Monetary Fund estimates that around 40 percent of jobs worldwide are now directly exposed to AI, a figure that already feels far too conservative. Where new technologies once mainly focused their efforts on doing away with the simple, mundane and repetitive tasks, AI has a grander objective. It is reaching into areas once thought untouchable, including and especially high-skill professions.

Advanced economies face the sharpest edge of this shift. It is expected that around 60% of jobs in these geographies will feel the impact first. For some people, the change could mean higher productivity and even higher incomes. For others, it will shrink demand for their expertise, push wages down and eventually eliminate their roles entirely.[VII] Indeed, the people that hold these roles may be entirely excluded from much of the prosperity AI promises. The result is a troubling polarisation in both wealth and opportunity. Inequality will soar within and between nations. For those who once believed that a nation's wealth and military power defined the greatest in global divides, AI represents a far more profound shift; a technological reset that will upend historically familiar power structures and usher in a new world order. The flip side of the coin is that emerging economies may be confronted by a different challenge altogether: They will likely dodge AI's first disruptive wave, but without the right infrastructure and skilled workers, they risk slipping impossibly far behind and unable to catchup.[VIII] Without targeted policies, such as retraining and educational programs alongside social safety nets, the ripple effects could deepen global inequality, turning progress itself into something hoarded by the wealthy.

Professions once thought untouchable by automation are proving to be easy pickings. Legal research that used to keep armies of junior associates busy is now handled more effectively, faster and more cheaply by platforms like ROSS Intelligence, ActionStep, and One Advanced. Financial analysts are watching a similar shift as AI chews through oceans of data in seconds, spitting out insights that once took researchers days. The result? Early-career tasks are vanishing, and with them the traditional stepping stones into white-collar industries.

Let's imagine a global manufacturing company that fully integrates AI into its supply chain. It will find it is able to immediately predict fluctuations in demand, automate its procurement decisions and thereafter, deploy an army of robots to optimise its factory production. At the surface, this appears to create an unprecedented efficiency. The stuff that all good, forward-thinking businesses are made of. But the ripple effects are far reaching. The speed of cost-cutting from one firm, will push competitors towards an uncomfortable choice; embrace similar technologies and lower prices, or face extinction altogether. Smaller firms will find themselves suffocated by a lethal combination of tech-poverty and an inability to compete on price, ultimately starting the countdown clock towards their complete disappearance. I'm not suggesting that this is in any way unfair, it's just one hypothetical business after all. However, this won't be limited to one business in one sector. The 'kill or be killed' question will be presented in one form or another to every business and across every sector. It is then that we will find that there is a larger cost. This consolidation of power will be the chief driver of economic inequality in the coming months, as smaller businesses are eliminated, leaving workers with fewer employment options and amplifying wealth concentration in the hands of a few corporate giants. This isn't theory, it's already well underway.

Agriculture faces a similar transformation. Beyond the automation we've already seen in machinery and harvesting; there is a quieter shift at work. AI-driven farming systems now monitor soil conditions, anticipate weather patterns, and time the planting and harvesting with remarkable precision. In this reality it is the largest agribusinesses that will thrive, producing food with record efficiency, while smallholders in emerging economies are left behind without the tools, knowledge, or capital to keep pace. Families that have worked the same land for generations, will suddenly find themselves priced out of the global markets that were once their livelihood. The imbalance won't just widen the economic divides; but will also exacerbate food security in regions that once relied on local harvests to survive.

And it isn't just factories and farms. Finance, once the lifeblood of the global economy, is being reshaped in ways that redefine risk and opportunity. New tools now parse news and market signals in real time, triggering trades at speeds no mortal being is able to match. Markets that once adjusted in minutes or hours now move in microseconds. Inefficiencies, historically the source of new opportunities, will disappear.

Benjamin Graham, the economist often cited as the father of value investing, famously personified the stock market as "Mr. Market," an emotional character prone to wild swings and misjudgements. In his 1949 publication 'The Intelligent Investor', the author explained that it was in human errors that investors could find the most profitable opportunities. But "Mr. Market" may now be heading for extinction too. Fundamentals will still matter, but their influence is being absorbed into prices with unprecedented speed.

Let's look at a hypothetical scenario. Imagine the fast-food chain Chick-fil-A announcing Sunday openings. This would be a development that would significantly expand revenues and profit prospects. Automated systems would be able to flood the order books before most people have even registered the headline, let alone reacted to it. The next layer of disruption is subtler. More importantly, these systems are not only reacting to headlines but interpreting the detail. A loss-making tech firm that reports worse than expected end of year results might normally see its stock plunge instantly. Yet if those same set of numbers were paired with a transformative growth statement, with fresh information signalling future profitability; AI would catch the nuance and reposition instantly, long before an analyst has read the statement. The real disruption lies not just in speed, but in the ability to read nuance at scale and consistency that no human can match. A looming geopolitical crisis could be scanned, not for its drama but for its economic fallout, with portfolios repositioned before most analysts have taken their first sip of Starbucks. With limited access to data and execution, retail investors may find themselves permanently outmanoeuvred by institutions that were often the architects of the AI they are using.

This dynamic is likely to drive consolidation across the investment industry itself. Opportunities that once sustained smaller funds are consumed instantly, leaving only scraps that are hardly enough to fund operational costs let alone deliver long-term returns for stakeholders. Thereafter, it is just a formality before this perfect storm compounds into a structural deficit: weaker results erode investor confidence, redemptions accelerate, and the cost of operating without cutting-edge AI becomes prohibitive. Being small is no longer a niche advantage but a liability. What emerges will be fewer, vastly larger funds. Their dominance won't rest on stock-picking genius but on computational supremacy: the monopoly of knowing true value first.

This is not speculation. Over the past two decades, hedge fund capital has concentrated in giants such as BlackRock and Vanguard, driven by economies of scale. AI will accelerate this gravitational pull, making it all but inevitable. This market consolidation isn't a new idea, but the speed and ferocity with which it's now coming will feel very new indeed. The industry that emerges won't look anything like the one we know today.

The real shift isn't just about survival. It's more about understanding what the market will start to reward. Once AI strips out inefficiency and scale crushes all competition, the game no longer revolves around spotting mis-priced assets. In the more entrepreneurial corners of the investment world, there will be a shift to specialise on earlier-stage ventures, where creativity, uncertainty and untested potential remain too ambiguous and nuanced for even the most advanced algorithms to quantify fully. In these nascent markets, human intuition, storytelling, and risk tolerance may retain a competitive edge, but even here, we will likely find that there is shelf life. AI's increasing ability to mimic and even surpass human creativity will threaten this frontier too; the days of AI unilaterally conceiving and birthing new disruptive enterprises is within touching distance and there will inevitably be (at least) a short-term opportunity for profit. Given the colossal shift that will take place across the way in which all businesses trade and operate, my expectation is that the financial markets will initially price in the phenomenal profit prospect and opportunity for AI efficiencies across all businesses, while ignoring the medium to longer term cost of AI.

Exactly how we arrive at this point is uncertain, but it will likely start with corporate announcements unveiling unprecedented levels of efficiency and increased margin. This in turn will trigger a repricing of the peers of that corporate in anticipation of a similarly positive earnings impact. There will, thereafter, be a moment of pause. How long the exuberance will last, or even estimating when it will start, is difficult to determine, but be assured, it will happen. This is of course a huge sweeping statement with very little specificity, but the bull market bubble we will see, is likely to dwarf the dot com boom of the late 90's. It will be during this phase, that the oracles among us will place their bets on when the inevitable, subsequent crash will follow. The period before that downward correction may be the last chance to position ourselves for a future defined by global-scale human redundancy, a moment to ask which assets will retain value when labour no longer underpins the economy.

The businesses that are able to reduce (or eliminate) the human element are poised to win big. However, the critical factor determining long-term success isn't just technological advantage. It will come down to whether businesses can grasp the urgency of aggressive customer acquisition now. This book sets out a number of predictions that are rarely discussed, and this is one of them: few are acknowledging just how decisive early customer capture will become in an AI-driven market. The reason is simple. AI doesn't just optimise operations, it homogenises them. As algorithms continue to converge on the same peak efficiency destination, with flawless logistics, optimal pricing and instant support; the outputs of these systems begin to look eerily similar. The margin for competitive differentiation narrows to nothing, except in one key area: the customer themselves. In this world of uniform optimisation, competitive advantage will no longer come from superior systems, but from owning the customer relationship first. Two equally optimised businesses offering near-identical products or services will leave customers with just one differentiating factor: brand familiarity.

Think of two burger chains offering a perfectly made cheeseburger. One is called "ABC Burgers," the other is McDonald's. Both use the same AI system, the same supply chain optimisation, the same price elasticity models. But only one has captured the customer. And in a frictionless environment, that customer relationship becomes incredibly hard to dislodge. This is why acquiring users today means acquiring them in perpetuity. The cost of acquisition is already spiralling, but so too is the long-term value of each customer. Churn rates will collapse as customers are locked into loyalty loops powered by personalised AI. Consumers are also likely to live much longer, compounding the lifetime value of each relationship. Spending heavily now may give the impression of strain on the balance sheet, yet every customer gained represents an enduring intangible asset. Hesitate, and the window will close forever.

We are, in effect, entering a full-scale customer acquisition arms race. Ambitious upstarts and legacy players alike will throw everything at building market share now because they understand what is at stake. I expect this shift to begin by the close of 2026, as the infrastructure, funding cycles, and AI maturity converge to make aggressive acquisition not just optional but inevitable. In many sectors, the outcome will be brutal. To borrow from the cult classic Highlander: in the end, there can be only one. Or at least, very few.

The very definition of opportunity is being rewritten, and investors as well as innovators must now adapt quickly. The question isn't whether these changes will occur but how quickly, and whether we as individuals, businesses, markets, and societies are ready to meet them. Ultimately, the bill for industrial-scale human redundancy will come due. Governments will have no choice but to shift the burden back onto the corporations that benefited most. We can expect new AI levies, automation taxes and eventually the rollout of some form of universal basic income. I believe this is unavoidable; once productivity becomes decoupled from employment, redistribution stops being a moral question and becomes an economic necessity. So, this won't be a question of political ideology but of survival. Without redistribution, entire economies will seize as consumption collapses. The precise path will differ country-by-country, but the trajectory is inevitable. The efficiency gains will deliver spectacular short-term profits and fuel temporary exuberance, but a darker reckoning will eventually arrive as millions displaced from work, demand systemic support. The irony is that the success of optimisation will force the state to intervene on a scale not seen since the post-war welfare settlement. Perhaps ever.

CHAPTER 2: THE EFFICIENCY TRAP

UBI and how we pay for what we consume is not the only shift ahead. The same technologies reshaping labour and value are also beginning to redefine the flow of energy, materials, and information that underpin every economy. Optimisation doesn't stop at payroll; it will become deeply entrenched into our supply chains, logistics, agriculture, and infrastructure too. It will change not just what we earn, but how we power, feed, and sustain ourselves. So perhaps it is a useful time to consider that cost. Training AI models consumes vast amounts of electricity and water for cooling. They are already straining energy grids, and our ecosystems are beginning to feel the pressure.[IX] A single model can emit more carbon than dozens of cars across their entire lifetimes. Data centres (the unseen engines of optimisation) are guzzling power on the scale of small nations.

What looks like efficiency in one domain can often create fragility in another. For example, electric vehicles promise lower emissions, yet the mining and refining of lithium and cobalt for their batteries leave deep ecological scars elsewhere. Yet even this environmentally costly phase is finite. The same optimisation power that drains resources, can also be repurposed toward planetary repair.

Climatologists are busily modelling weather extremes with greater precision, giving affected areas the valuable time needed to prepare for floods, wildfires, and droughts. Simulations of atmospheric and ocean systems allow scientists to test theoretical climate interventions without risk, from carbon sequestration to geoengineering. Energy and infrastructure are at the front line of this shift. Algorithms can balance power grids in real time, reduce waste in solar and wind distribution, whilst optimising transport systems to reduce fuel and water consumption.[X] Each of these applications hints at a future where technology is not solely a consumer of our resources, but an essential cog in the solution wheel. The same technology that gorges on our energy supplies today could help us manage it more intelligently tomorrow.

The instinct of self-preservation is natural. Faced with disruption, we might ask: How do I protect my job, my savings, my business? It's the fight-or-flight reflex reframed in economic form. But jobs won't be picked off one at a time. This is a fundamental reset that is redrawing the entire ocean in which those roles, our savings and businesses even make sense in the first place. When entire industries, cultures and monetary systems collapse, the waves reach all of us. Even if your own role is spared in the shorter term, the greater turbulence will reach you anyway. Perhaps a doctor, a lawyer, a plumber will be fine for the immediate term. But, collapsing markets, shrinking tax bases, disrupted supply and the psychological fallout of mass displacement will destabilise our lives far more profoundly than the loss of our own source of income ever could. The cruel truth is this: the thing we may try to defend (our personal slice of stability) only holds value so long as the wider system around us is coherent and functional. Protecting "me" is futile if "us" dissolves.

History has shown us this pattern before. During the banking and housing crisis of 2008, plenty of people kept their jobs, but still watched as their pensions and house values imploded. During the pandemic, those of us that avoided infection still endured the lockdowns and broken supply chains. Time and again, the greater danger arrives indirectly. The threat we face is not confined to the replacement of "me" but instead to the collapse of "us."

Chapter 3: Behind the Curtain

> *Orwell probably would not have known what to make of X (Twitter), but he would have recognised the trick. In 1984 he imagined governments twisting truth with propaganda. Today it is lines of code, not party slogans, that determine what headlines we're exposed to, which video clips will keep us hooked when we should have gone to bed an hour ago. Linger on one post and suddenly everything you see begins to sound the same. The unsettling truth is that we have built the walls of this echo chamber ourselves.*

Information now moves at such a velocity, that it invites clutter. Streams of stories, adverts, and minor diversions are published each and every second, all of which are vying to win the attention of our social feeds. This barrage of content creates the potential for a deafening amount of confusion and noise, which serves neither readers nor the platforms that rely on repeat engagement. It is here that the interests of both the social media giants and its consumers begin to align: both sides need better sorting. This is where filtering steps in, promising order. At first it feels useful. The filtering is almost like having a friend flick through a newspaper for articles that might appeal. Yet that same filtering 'friend' shapes the bubble we live in and entrenches the opinions that grow inside it. There can't be many of us that haven't opened YouTube with humble ambitions to watch a single clip, only to find ourselves still there an hour later, drifting from one video to the next. The logic is simple: what we watch, when we pause and where we click, tells the system what to serve us next. It works uncannily well because we are the ones that have trained it. It is undoubtedly seductive, but it leaves us facing a bigger question. As we're not choosing freely, who (or what) is making the choices for us?

The largest social networks are built to thrive on this cycle. Facebook, Instagram and TikTok code their algorithms to analyse our preferences, behaviours, and interactions. They pinpoint the precise moment at which we are most engaged with a piece of material, or conversely least enthused. It is an addictive feedback loop, where the more we engage with it, the more we are served similar content.

Consider how quickly a passing interest can quickly spiral into an obsession. How watching a fitness video can suddenly fill a social media feed with workout routines. Or how idly clicking an article about luxury travel triggers a cascade of exotic getaways and designer luggage ads. Even a quick search for unique interior design concepts could morph into an avalanche of furniture recommendations and DIY hacks. We are served more of whatever we consume. There is a darker side too, though. Someone viewing conspiracy theories or politically charged speeches, may soon notice their feed shift to reinforce those perspectives. The result is one where our bias is amplified and alternative views are shut out.

The political consequences have been well documented. During the 2016 U.S. presidential election, Facebook provoked outrage over the distribution of divisive political ads targeted at specific voter groups. It has been well reported that many of these campaigns were (allegedly) orchestrated by foreign actors in an attempt to sway public opinion.[XI] Similarly, during the UK's referendum on EU membership, some reports highlighted how targeted ads were used to push exaggerated claims to influence undecided voters. Algorithms, optimised for engagement rather than truth, can turn a passing curiosity into a barrage of content that distorts reality, creating a fertile environment for misinformation campaigns to develop and thrive.

The darker side of this invisible puppeteer lies outside of politics. Anti-vaccine misinformation was amplified during the pandemic in similar ways. A study published in the British Medical Journal criticised Facebook and Twitter (X) for their inadequate response to false claims about vaccines. The platforms tend to prioritise posts based on engagement, regardless of the content's evidence.....or lack thereof.[XII] A more chilling example still, lies in the phenomenon of suicide echo-chambers. Engaging with content about depression or mental health struggles has been shown to lead to social feeds increasingly populated by posts and videos that almost romanticise suicidal ideation.[XIII] Desperately unhelpful for the vulnerable individuals who often find themselves the principal consumers of this content. Although these cases just scratch the surface of the wider issue, they demonstrate how social networks can sometimes contribute to tragedy, validating the darkest thoughts at the worst possible time. Designed to maximise engagement, the algorithms elect to ignore when their recommendations shift to being a source of dangerous reinforcement. And it is here that we find the need for urgent, ethical guardrails in our digital spaces.

One might think that given this evidence, the leaders of the chief offending organisations might show some contrition. However, it is these same figures that have been remarkably effective at shaping how we think about responsibility. Mark Zuckerberg, Sam Altman, and Elon Musk have each published open letters and research papers that on the surface, sound like stark warnings about the dangers of their own creations.[XIV] At first sight, this candour appears noble, as if they are inviting us all into the problem-solving process. The subtext is more cunning, however. The reframing of this conversation into one of shared responsibility has the effect of creating an illusion of transparency, almost excusing the absence of real safety nets. No one is policing them, so they police themselves, but only after the fact. In many of the instances of tragedy, as in the case of Molly Russell (whose exposure to harmful online content ended in suicide), the response tends to be diplomacy. Apologies are swiftly followed with the promise of new resources and the now well-rehearsed script of tech giants pledging to do better.[XV] The cruel genius of the approach is that the acknowledgement of failure becomes a kind of shield, with apologies replacing accountability and promises of future improvement distracting from the absence of pre-emptive measures. It is policing by apology. Ultimately, we are left with a system where the power remains with the people that built the infrastructure that caused the harm in the first place.

These tragedies are not outliers. Internal research from Meta revealed that Instagram worsened body image issues for one in three teenage girls who used the platform.[XVI] The acknowledgment was stark, yet even then it was framed as something to be managed rather than prevented. Little has changed since. The same algorithms continue to shape behaviour, quietly amplifying the insecurities that keep people coming back.

It is also these same algorithms that dictate the soundtracks to our lives. Popular consumer facing platforms like Spotify and YouTube deliver us music and video recommendations based on our past choices. Aside from the inequities of royalty distribution they have spawned, they are widely considered a highly desirable deployment of machine learning technologies. But even on occasions when this personalisation introduces us to new favourites, it more often narrows our exposure, creating an "algorithmic bubble" that limits our musical and cultural horizons. Spotify's "Discover Weekly" playlist is a case in point. It analyses a user's listening history to generate personalised recommendations. While undeniably accurate in pinpointing new likely favourites, many have found the system simply reinforces existing preferences. YouTube delivers similarly calculated recommendations too, often guiding users down familiar rabbit holes of content, that work to subtly discourage exploration. All very well if its acoustic covers of Beatles classics, but when it comes to fringe political material, it surely raises deeper questions over who controls what we do and do not have access to. A 2020 study found that Facebook users were more likely to encounter news and opinions that reinforced the views espoused by their preferred political affiliations, which some may argue, deepens polarisation. [XVII] These platforms are designed to maximise watch time, and they succeed. If they spread misinformation, it's because our attention is so easily grabbed by sensationalism. They are mirrors that show us a distorted but revealing image of ourselves. And it's not an especially attractive one.

These trends are not confined to fringe political clips, music or film, but reach into every part of the information we see and share. Disinformation has become an increasingly familiar weapon of cyberwarfare. From falsified news reports to armies of bots posting false information during armed conflicts, the lines that separate propaganda and attack have been blurred. Democracies that have been built on the slow churn of debate are particularly vulnerable to this shift, where an election can be influenced by terabytes of quickly distributed, fabricated persuasion flowing through our social feeds. Orwell's prophetic nightmare of state propaganda has mutated into something far more treacherous: A battlefield where the truth itself is the primary casualty.

Because we have ceded control of what we consume, we are now more at risk of becoming passive participants in our own realities. Sculpted by systems that prioritise engagement over distributing verifiably true content; the invisible puppeteers that once appeared harmless, are being manipulated to pull at the strings of our autonomy. If we are to reclaim control, we must first recognise how subtly (and completely) these algorithms already shape the world we see.

Chapter 4: The Cost of Perfect Health

> *What would Florence Nightingale make of a healthcare system in which machines are making the life and death decisions, rather than people? A fierce advocate for patient centred care, she is credited with a nursing revolution that insisted on data driven decision making, an approach that eerily mirrors AI's strengths. Nightingale saw medicine as both science and an art, where a care-giver's intuition and bedside manner were as vital as numbers. Would she welcome the precision delivered by machine learning as the next logical step in medical evolution, or despair at care delivered via data points on a screen?*

Like most large health systems, the NHS is drowning in inefficiencies. Patient demand outpaces staff and resources, and waitlists are not an issue that can be fixed by money alone. The brutal truth is that the health service is structurally addicted to sick people. Funding, estates, staffing structures and performance metrics reward diagnosing and treating illness, not preventing it. We can count prescriptions and procedures. We can't count the people who never get sick. This moment is not just an opportunity for marginal improvement, but a chance to reset how healthcare will be delivered. If we get this right, it could finally make care efficient, more precise and accessible, and crucially, highly scalable.

The transition from human-led medicine to technology-assisted and ultimately machine-directed care is loaded with tension. In the UK, the health service is fiercely protected as a national symbol. No politician dares criticise it without consequence, and change is resisted even when urgently needed; a symptom of fear largely driven by the fact that health is the mother of all political hot potatoes.

Medicine has always been defined by judgment, trust, and experience, so the idea of algorithms replacing any of these, almost feels like an indignity. The shift will be cultural as much as technological, and it will likely be met with scepticism and a large dose of hostility. There won't be a question mark surrounding the capability of technology, but as healthcare has historically been about people caring for people, the change will feel somewhat counter intuitive. And so, it's unlikely that the transformation will come in one sweeping move. It will likely begin at the edges: supporting GPs with faster diagnosis, helping radiologists and pathologists detect anomalies and refining treatment pathways. But what begins as support, will soon evolve and expand into selecting cancer treatments from global data, guiding robotic surgery, and transforming triage into something predictive rather than reactive.

The first tangible gains are starting to emerge, with an early impact already evident in radiology, pathology, and blood analysis. When trained on specialist-reviewed cases, systems have been successfully screening out normal results, whilst highlighting anomalies that need closer attention. Looking beyond diagnostics, the most pressing opportunity lies at the literal front door of the NHS, where emergency departments absorb a disproportionate share of resources. Machine-assisted triage could safely manage low-risk patients and help clear queues. Even these small efficiencies will compound quickly: for example, saving just one minute per attendance at a hospital the size of St Thomas' in Westminster would free up more than a hundred clinician-days over the course of a year.

Public debate often dwells on distant transformation, but the most immediate role for these intelligent systems is in relieving legacy strain. At first this will look like temporary fixes, easing pain points without addressing the underlying structure. Over time though, the limits of surface improvements become clearer, confidence grows, and pressure builds for more substantive change, until incremental adjustments give way to something closer to open surgery at the heart of the system.

Waiting lists are a prime example. Intelligent systems could reorder priority

CHAPTER 4: THE COST OF PERFECT HEALTH

so those most in need are seen on demand, in real time. Static queues driven by inaccurate data would give way to models that continually reassess patients and reorder priorities based on the degree of urgency rather than process. This lays the groundwork for prevention, predicting illness before it occurs, intervening early, and creating treatments tailored to individual biology. At first the change will feel slow, then the pace quickens until the system seems to shift all at once. The result is not just faster and more accurate care, but an increase in healthy life that is broadly shared rather than exclusively for the wealthy.

These tools already exist and are saving lives in limited settings. Machine learning has shown how analysing millions of medical records can reveal patterns in how illness develops, spreads, and responds to care, insights that were previously too complex or too vast for the human eye to detect. It can redistribute staffing resources more effectively than any administrator confronted with a stack of paperwork. Tasks that may once have relied on a bank of clerical staff, can be automated, shortening delays and freeing clinician time to focus on what matters most. Early cancer detection has been validated against radiologist review, cardiovascular models are reducing invasive procedures,[XVIII] and during the COVID pandemic; outbreak modelling and mapping of protein structures outpaced those announced via the daily government broadcasts. The irony is that healthcare does not need to wait for intelligent systems to arrive. They are already here, and there is no reason not to deploy them more aggressively. The obstacles are bureaucratic rather than technical, cultural rather than scientific. Resistance is not about safety concerns, it's about ownership.

Digital pathology was ready for a decade before adoption,[XIX] but pathologists resisted for fear of being centralised into irrelevance. A smartphone tool capable of diagnosing venous thrombosis[XX] in emergency departments stalled because radiology claimed ownership of the condition.[XXI] These turf wars show that innovation in healthcare does not fail because of insufficient tools, but because the question of who is wielding the power, is contested.

The breakthroughs ahead are not exclusively about incremental efficiency or catching cancers earlier. The cumulative impact of all these improvements happening at once, is what will deliver the radical change. That said, there are some insanely exciting developments at the fringes of healthcare. New discoveries promise not just marginal gains, but potentially transformative shifts in how we think about ageing itself. Scientists are experimenting with reversing the epigenome, switching genetic programs back to the youthful settings we carried in our twenties.[XXII] If these switches can be reliably flipped, ageing ceases to be an inevitable decline and becomes a condition to be treated. Animal and primate trials suggest this is not fantasy but imminent reality, and some of the best-funded ventures on earth are racing to deliver it to humans.[XXIII]

As these possibilities emerge, the question ceases to be one about capability and becomes more a case of willingness. Hesitation so often proves to be the costliest danger. There is a considerable risk that early advances are slowed by an insistence on rigid guidelines and established protocols; safer, perhaps, but at the cost of embracing transformative change in its fullest form. Innovation in healthcare has often relied on serendipity, creativity, or a hunch followed against the prevailing winds of wisdom. Few areas illustrate this tension between caution and boldness as vividly as regenerative medicine. One of its most remarkable breakthroughs is stem cell rejuvenation. At birth we carry a vast army of stem cells, only for stocks to dwindle by orders of magnitude by our mid-40s. New ventures are now commercialising ways to restore these reserves, and the early signs look promising. Studies have shown stem-cell-derived injectables can reduce inflammation and pain, and in some cases even rebuild muscle mass without the need for exercise. Sign me up. If these findings can be scaled, conditions once seen as inevitable markers of ageing such as arthritis, sarcopenia, and immune decline may one day be treated as reversible ailments rather than lifelong burdens.[XXIV]

Research is moving quickly in nanotechnology and advanced modelling too. In medicine, nanotechnology refers to engineering materials at a scale smaller than a human cell, allowing treatments to be delivered with extraordinary precision. Imagine particles designed to seek out and repair damaged tissue or target tumours from within the bloodstream. Advanced modelling, meanwhile, uses enormous datasets and computing power to simulate how the body behaves at the molecular level, helping us understand complex biological systems in ways that were once impossible. Quantum simulations are now bringing us closer to predicting billions of cellular reactions per second, pointing to a future where we can create digital replicas of organs and, eventually, entire people.[XXV]

Far from speculative, these breakthroughs are already influencing how we discover and test new medicines. Intelligent systems are being deployed to map protein structures, design new antibiotics and predict aspects of a drug's safety before it ever enters the body. Virtual trials may never entirely replace human testing, but modelling is beginning to compress timelines from years to months while refining participant selection and diagnostic precision. Unlike health systems that can resist change for cultural reasons, drug companies are driven by the time it takes to reach the market. For this reason, novel drug discovery is likely to be one of the first areas where machine learning is more than a tool, becoming the foundation of something truly transformational.

All of this cascades toward the most audacious yet credible prospect: longevity escape velocity. This is the moment when for every twelve months lived, science extends life by more than a year.[XXVI] In practice it means death itself could be postponed, perhaps indefinitely. To many this sounds fantastical, but the science points unmistakably in that direction. If discovery continues at the present pace, and if interventions to reset cells, replenish stem stocks, and repair DNA continue to succeed, then lifespans of 150, 200 and beyond are no longer miraculous but mechanical. Mortality begins to look less like destiny and more like a solvable problem.

Progress toward longer, healthier lives is unlikely to be opposed in principle, yet the adoption of new tools that make it possible will meet strong resistance within healthcare itself. Highly trained clinicians who have spent decades mastering care will champion caution, citing specific case failures and emphasising the need for independent judgment and one-to-one care. These arguments deserve respect. Failures have occurred, and skewed data has produced uneven results.[XXVII] Early deployments that misclassified conditions or failed with marginalised groups are warnings that clearly cannot be dismissed or casually explained away. They emphasise the need for rich data, oversight, and humility in deployment. For example, healthcare datasets already over-represent white, middle-aged men. The risk of deepening existing biases rather than correcting them only grows if we continue to train the data uncritically. This isn't just an ethical concern, but a safety one. And when those biases translate into outcomes, it is people who carry the consequences, not the machines that generated them. For clinicians, failure is personal, a life lost is a family bereaved. For algorithms, failure is statistical; it will learn from the outcome, but there will be no grief, merely a digital reflection of whether an error rate is considered acceptable. When the acceptable includes real tragedies, accountability blurs. Whose responsibility is that death: the algorithm, the clinician, or the system that approved its use?

Physicians are likely to retain a central function for the immediate future, but there is little doubt that their roles will have to change. Where they are not architects of the new technologies, they will evolve into interpreters of complex outputs, patient advocates, and ethical overseers. Yet there is a smaller group going further. Some of the most promising initiatives are being shaped by visionary clinicians.

Recognising that algorithms cannot succeed in isolation; collaborations between psychiatrists and machine learning researchers have matched therapies to an individual's genetic, behavioural and social profile.[XXVIII] It's all part of a richer plan to personalise mental health interventions. Meanwhile, oncologists at the Royal Marsden in London, have been testing adaptive radiotherapy protocols that adjust in real time to a tumour's response.[XXIX] These doctors see the chance to improve outcomes not by clinging to legacy pathways but by placing themselves at the centre of future-focused care. They may be few, but their influence will endure long after others have been replaced and even after intelligent systems are fully established. In the end, those who choose to lead this change are the ones who will still have a place within it.

The work of these pioneers is reinforced by the lessons of the pandemic, when the potential of intelligent systems was tested in real time. Protein structure prediction handed scientists insights into viral proteins, facilitating the rapid development of vaccines at a time when traditional techniques would have taken months;[XXX] Predictive analytics identified patients most at risk of severe outcomes and helped hospitals allocate scarce beds and ventilators; Early warning systems flagged an unusual pneumonia outbreak well before official alerts were able to confirm it.[XXXI] What emerged was a blueprint for the future. Systems that spanned the full chain of response allowed resources to be more optimally managed by spotting the threat and speeding the path to prevention.

What followed the pandemic has been a global experiment in adoption. The same technologies that transformed crisis response are now revealing both the strengths and weaknesses of national health systems. In Singapore, where digital records are unified and national identity infrastructures are tightly woven; new systems have slipped into healthcare almost seamlessly, helping to automate triage, re-order waiting lists and guide decision making without the need for endless debate.[XXXII] Efficiency is just assumed.

CHAPTER 4: THE COST OF PERFECT HEALTH

It is surprising that in the United States, a very different story is unfolding. Healthcare is perpetually held back by fragmented legacy systems that refuse to connect. Patient data is scattered across multiple providers and states like shards of a broken mirror. Each piece shows an incomplete picture; a confusing, warped reflection that is of little value in the pursuit of optimal patient outcomes. The system sparkles in parts yet collapses in others. It only goes to show that even with the most advanced tools, a structure built to resist unification cannot be saved.

Which brings the question home: what would it mean for artificial intelligence to fully integrate into the NHS, and could that unlock an advantage few others can match? Full integration is less a switch than a threshold. We will know that we've crossed it when triage, scheduling, staffing, and risk models are all informed by the same learning system; when measurable improvements in access, outcomes, cost, and consistency become clear. The NHS is often criticised for its bulk and bureaucracy, yet its centralised structure and colossal scale give it something rare.... a unified data estate linked to a single payer and a single set of objectives. If privacy and governance are handled with care, that estate is a strategic asset of global significance. It could allow the NHS to move its objectives from reactive care to anticipatory care faster than fragmented systems. In that scenario, the very attributes once seen as liabilities become strengths and assets. A national platform can learn once and benefit all. A free at the point of use mandate aligns with the efficiencies of scale that intelligent systems deliver, and cost pressure will eventually push every system in that direction anyway. The real prize lies in unlocking the model of perfect healthcare; whoever achieves it first will hold a currency of unparalleled value, one that can be exported worldwide. If the UK chooses to lead here, the NHS could quickly find itself at the forefront of this shift.

None of this negates the need to confront the risk. In countries where for-profit healthcare models shape access, optimisation for revenue rather than need will likely deepen divides. Even within the federalised systems that are able to pool vast amounts of patient data, models trained on distorted historical statistics can still reproduce past unfairness. Without an appropriately vigilant approach, algorithms can embed existing inequalities into their decision-making. This risks leaving certain patient groups consistently worse off. These concerns do not undermine the promise, but they do place a firm burden of responsibility on those who build, regulate, and deploy it.

Elderly care shows both hope and challenge. In recent years, smartwatches and fitness trackers have become common tools for monitoring health, whilst more specialised wearable devices are now extending that idea into assisted living. Products like CarePredict track changes in movement and routine to flag signs of decline before a crisis occurs. Bedside sensors such as EarlySense are now well established, monitoring vital signs on a continuous basis and alerting caregivers to any sudden changes. But these products are only scratching the surface of what's going to be possible over the coming months.[xxxiii] In hospitals across the United States, Diligent Robotics has enjoyed early success from the deployment of Moxi, a robot that is quickly making itself a critical part of clinical life, running pharmacy errands and transporting samples. Alongside them, fleets of Aethon TUG robots carry meals, linens and medical supplies through wards and corridors. Meanwhile, the EksoNR exoskeleton is now helping patients stand and walk far earlier after stroke or spinal cord injury, reducing strain and improving recovery outcomes.[xxxiv] These are no longer pilot studies but active deployments, proof that robotics can relieve strain while returning time and dignity to human care.

What lies ahead is moving faster still. Sanctuary AI is advancing tactile sensing so that a robot can feel the weight and texture of what it holds, an innovation that could allow machines to guide a person's arm or prevent a fall without harm.[xxxv] In Japan, a purpose-built test community called 'Woven City', launched in 2025 and is now serving as a real-world testing ground for domestic robotics.[xxxvi] Inside its homes, ceiling-mounted manipulators, mobile service bots and responsive kitchens are being trialled as extensions of human capability rather than replacements for it. A potential game-changer for assisted living environments. But as robotics redefine the mechanics of care, they also invite scrutiny of the quieter, human dimensions that technology cannot yet quantify.

Medicine has long balanced two forms of 'knowing'. The first is the data that can be measured, the second is the stories that patients tell; how did the symptoms begin, how has illness affected work, or more pertinently, how do they feel. Intelligent systems push healthcare firmly toward the former. Probabilities and numbers replace narrative. While this strengthens population health, it risks eroding the therapeutic relationship rooted in listening to a patient's story. The danger is that people become datapoints, as opposed to partners in their own recovery. Renowned surgeon and policy maker Atul Gawande has written that the goal of medicine is not only health and survival but enabling well-being.[xxxvii] Yet well-being itself is difficult to define or measure, and the tension between extending life and safeguarding its quality grows sharper in the space between technologies built for populations and people who long to be recognised as more than a number. It is in that space where the outliers, rare conditions, and fragile patient narratives can disappear too easily.

As these new intelligent systems become our healers, we run the risk of forgetting what it means to care and to be cared for. Although I suspect that will be a transitory memory that quickly fades, replaced by a new contract of trust. It really won't take long for us to place our confidence in carers that do not tire, falter, or fail. The prospect of outstanding healthcare that is delivered immediately is too attractive to resist. Reliability and precision will become the new currencies of comfort and compassion. The next phase of medicine will dissolve the boundaries between care and daily life. Healthcare will no longer be a destination but a condition of existence, continuous, ambient and responsive. It will live in your watch, your phone, the ring on your finger, the autonomous drug delivery patch on your arm, the intelligent prosthetic, the evolving diet, the personalised supplement, and the instant diagnosis delivered before symptoms even appear. Treatment will arrive without appointment or delay, guided by systems that anticipate rather than react. The body itself will become the interface, constantly measured, adjusted and refined. This is not a distant vision but an accelerating reality, one that redefines what it means to be well. And the consequence of these compounding advances is a relentless trajectory: the first multi-centenarian has almost certainly already been born. The pace of discovery makes such longevity less fantasy than inevitability.

Nightingale, the great reformer of data-driven care, would likely have urged us to embrace this progress rather than resist it. And assuming that this progress is inevitable, then education in the healthcare field faces the far sharper edge of the disruption dilemma. Healthcare will change far faster than the curriculum can. I would go as far to say that setting out on a five-year course now risks almost complete obsolescence before graduation. Anyone beginning a medical degree today will graduate into a profession utterly transformed from the one they set out to join. This isn't because medicine will disappear, it won't, but because it will evolve into something unrecognisable to what we have today. My plea to those who work in the healthcare space is simple: embrace new tools willingly. Resist defending the old order. In doing so you will preserve the art of care while capturing the certainty that in this domain, the future gets better, and gets better fast.

DEAR FUTURE: YOU CAN KEEP THE CHANGE

Chapter 5: Chalkboards & Chatbots

> *Walk into a Montessori classroom a century ago and you'd likely find mats on the floor as small hands sort through wooden letters; Children turning sounds into words as their teacher stands back, present and observing, but mostly silent. The idea was a simple one: School should revolve around a child's own instincts. Maria Montessori resisted uniformity. She wanted children to discover and learn by instinct, following their personal interests with playful experimentation. Now, over a century later, that vision feels strangely familiar as the prospect of personalised learning finally moves within our grasp. But I suspect Montessori would still be cautious. Technology might help a child bloom, but it can just as easily reduce learning to targets and tick box exercises.*

I will make no secret of my anger for how badly education has let students down for decades. To this very day, most classrooms still feel like factories in a disguise. A teacher stands at the front, with rows of desks lined up in uniform rows as students are marched through the exact same material, at the same pace. It's a structure that serves those that fit the mould very well indeed, but is equally effective at ostracising those who don't. The result is an education system that tells children that their uniqueness doesn't matter and if anything, is desperately inconvenient. More painful still is that it ultimately becomes a problem for the child to deal with alone. And yet, all the while we have known that no two children are the same. So why have we persisted in thinking they could all learn in the same way?

One of my own children thrives in creative tasks, forever inventing fantastical new worlds and creatures that live within them, building dens by finding new life for old Amazon delivery boxes. Another thrives on logic, actually enjoying the formulaic learning that has been prescribed to her and relishing the prospect of an exam paper being marked. One fits neatly into the existing educational mould, the other clearly does not. But both are forced to march in lockstep with the same system that neither recognises nor rewards their differences. It's a big problem.

The damage to children that don't fit in, is impossible to deny. Curiosity fades as the lights of learning gradually dim into a soft flicker. Gifts that might have grown into a tangible skill, a creative talent or perhaps even a new vocation never previously considered, are left withering and unexplored. But there's a contrast. Just as the shouts for educational reform reach their loudest, AI arrives with the potential to do exactly that. If implemented wisely, new learning platforms would finally allow education to evolve around each child's unique pace of learning, catering to their strengths and amplifying their promise.

The shift is already happening. ChatGPT has begun full integration with external applications, allowing anyone to say, "I want to learn quantum mechanics," or "Teach me the history of Renaissance art," and within seconds it can generate a complete, structured curriculum with progressive modules, readings, and practical exercises. The learner can then engage with the material in real time, not only through written responses but also by voice, holding a living conversation that adapts as understanding deepens. This is more than convenience. It marks the arrival of a tutor available to anyone, anywhere, at any moment. It's a teacher that never tires, forgets, or judges. It can break down complex ideas into smaller steps, provide metaphors that strengthen understanding, and adjust the pace and tone to suit each learner's curiosity and level of skill. What traditional education has long promised but rarely delivered, genuine personalisation, is now emerging as a working reality. The implications are enormous. Studies already show that conversational AI systems can raise student engagement and retention far beyond standardised instruction.[xxxviii] Integrations linking large-language-model platforms to coding environments, image tools, and live web data mean education can now move beyond static textbooks toward genuinely interactive learning. Students will not just learn from these systems but with them, questioning, refining, and co-creating knowledge in ways that mirror how experts think and teach.

CHAPTER 5: CHALKBOARDS & CHATBOTS

In practice, though, change has been underway for quite some time. And maybe this shouldn't be too much of a surprise. After all, it didn't first arrive via policy or curriculum reform, but instead it crept in, driven by the viral spread of chatbot tools the rest of us have been growing increasingly dependent on. Over the past 4 years in particular, they've changed how young people learn. In 2024, surveys showed that more than eight in ten students were leveraging AI to assist in their studies.[xxxix] Sometimes it is in a supporting role, like summarising an article and occasionally for ideation or polishing a draft. But often (more problematically), for completing assignments at home. This has raised legitimate concerns around academic honesty and plagiarism. It is no longer a tool operating at the obscure edges of schooling; it is embedded into the very heart of how students complete their work. And so, whilst the classroom still looks much the same, learning has been redefined by the devices that live in the students' pockets.

Institutions are now beginning to follow where students once led. Nearly half of U.S. schools already report using AI in some shape or form. And the trend is accelerating. Analysts project the global AI in education market will grow from the $5.9 billion it stands at today to $32 billion within the next four years. That surge in capital isn't abstract; it's funding very real changes in classrooms. Whilst the earliest applications have focused on administrative matters such as grading and tutoring support, the potential reach is far deeper. AI has already begun to predict the risk of a student dropping out by flagging those that are less engaged, long before teachers might have noticed.[XL] It's also analysing test results in real time, mapping patterns that help educators evolve lesson plans around struggling students. These are not fringe pilots but signals of a structural shift in what "schooling" itself means.

Before we start to move the furniture around, we should ask the only real question that matters: what is education for? We have treated school as the first step of a processing line that manufactures workers; embark on study, graduate, then get a job. That formular is broken. In field after field, machines already outperform us. So, what are we preparing children for if the role they train toward might vanish or shrink before they even arrive?

Walk through a radiology department at a tech-led hospital and you'll likely find software catching tumours that senior clinicians miss. Where does that leave a newly qualified doctor; empathy and bedside manner? Six years of training cannot rest on small talk. In engineering there is a similar story.

Software designs, tests, and stress-checks faster than teams of graduates can. And so, the human element has to shift. We have to become the ethical backstop, the collaborator; ultimately, we need to be the support function rather than the lead. If education does not adapt to that reality, we will keep training people for roles the world no longer needs. We need to redefine the goal. Not "education for employment," but "education for a life that keeps changing." That means thinking clearly, adapting and learning how to live well when roles shift beneath our feet. Teach the basics, but then make room for what cannot be standardised or taught: nurture growth in imagination, a sense of humour, empathy, the talents that make one child different from the next. This is where AI could be transformative. Imagine classrooms where the curriculum adapts to the child. AI enabled tutors can observe how a student learns, where and when they struggle, what excites them. The pacing and style of education adapts, offering multiple routes into mastering a subject, and suggesting projects that fit their strengths and curiosities. The bird-mad kid does ratios on migration data. A budding guitarist would learn to hear patterns in sound before tackling equations. The curriculum stays rigorous, but the road to it stops being a single lane.

Recent classroom pilots point the same way. Microsoft's most recent 'AI in Education' report captured the shift vividly, with students reporting a sense of greater ownership over their learning when AI tools were part of the process.[XLI] Instead of passively receiving instruction, they found themselves as co-creators of a custom teaching plan, more engaged in setting their own goals and able to measure progress. Teachers reported a higher level of motivation, especially among those who had previously switched off. It was as though the machinery of education had finally begun to see the humanity inside the student, rather than forcing the student to adapt to a tired process.

We're now starting to see the early signs of scale in real world deployments too. At Alpha School in Texas, students are already learning without teachers. Guided entirely by AI powered tablets and laptops, lessons are personalised through gamification and eye-tracking, whilst the learning is responsive, adapting its pacing to ensure the student is keeping up. Test scores have shown students landing in the 90th percentile while slashing academic hours to just two per day.[XLII] Further afield in Beijing, AI education has become a compulsory component of the curriculum, ensuring every child has a baseline familiarity with the tools that will reshape their future. These classrooms have become laboratories of state-backed AI, where headbands can also track concentration through EEG signals, uniforms are chipped to record attendance, and algorithms generate minute-by-minute reports for teachers and parents.[XLIII] In Australia, public schools are deploying EduChat, an AI system tied to the national syllabus, helping students refine essays and expand critical thinking while guarding against plagiarism.[XLIV] Meanwhile in India, AI is being adopted across mainstream and city schools, with thousands of CBSE institutions now teaching artificial intelligence, coding, and robotics as part of the core curriculum. At the same time, Hi-Tech labs are bringing the same opportunities to rural children who might otherwise never have touched a computer. No one is being left behind; the transformation is reaching classrooms in both urban centres and remote communities alike.[XLV]

What began in primary and secondary schools is now making rapid inroads into higher education too. At Arizona State University, an AI-powered system called 'Jill Watson' has been answering student questions in online forums for years, often with a greater consistency than teaching assistants.[XLVI] At Carnegie Learning, maths software is generating personalised problems for students, ensuring that more time is spent in the zone between comfort and frustration, where learning is richest. In South Korea, the education software firm 'Riiid' offers AI tutoring apps that continuously adapt to a student's progress, producing measurable improvements in test preparation outcomes. [XLVII] These examples show the diversity of AI's impact: tutoring and guidance built around a supportive scaffold. Different tools, but delivering the same aim of making teaching responsive, not robotic.

And so, it really isn't a difficult stretch to imagine a time where each and every student has a learning companion, a kind of intellectual exoskeleton that adjusts and adapts as they grow. But even that future wouldn't mean teachers disappear overnight. Schools are more than knowledge delivery systems. They are environments where children figure out friendships, cope with conflict, develop resilience and empathy in the messy company of others. They are places of safety as much as instruction, where parents entrust not just their child's education but their care, supervision, and socialisation. Parents rely on that as much as grades.

Within this shifting landscape, the traditional teaching role will have to evolve. AI has shown its mettle in shouldering the heavy lifting of delivering lessons, drilling facts, and tailoring exercises to each child's pace. But for now, it cannot set values, model character, or offer a sense of belonging. A good teacher ties ideas together, shows why they matter, and offers the patience and encouragement that turn information into understanding. They will more often act as mentors than instructors, focusing on shaping curiosity and modelling the judgment that turns information into knowledge. In the first instance, the teaching role is not diminished by AI, but rather liberated from the grind of vanilla instruction so that they can focus on the deeper work of nurturing a child's true potential. Yet it would be naïve to imagine this phase as permanent, but rather a transitional opening act of a revolution in education. It is difficult to see a future where ultimately, machines not only claim ownership of the delivery of knowledge but, one day, the role of mentor itself.

There is also the matter of homework. With AI tools now just a click away, there is an uncomfortably fine line between a legitimate helping hand and something that crosses the threshold of cheating. Given some 86 percent of students are using AI as a study aid,[XLVIII] we surely need a rethink about what homework is for. If a learning assignment is about the ability to recall facts, a bot will win every time. It's time to change the brief. We need to ask students for their reflections, insist on real world experiments, whilst encouraging the development of personal voice; work that requires judgement, not just asking questions and expecting answers. The process of assessment must now evolve in line with the tools.

In higher education, a quiet identity crisis is taking shape. As AI is emerging as both the expert and the gatekeeper, the role of these institutions will be forced to evolve too. Universities, which were built to promote and preserve knowledge, will have to redefine what it means to create it. Many will repurpose as lifelong learning destinations, offering micro-credentials and fluid courses that can be taken at any age. Others will morph into civic hubs, where it will be less about delivering and unpacking knowledge, and more about cultivating the kind of reflective, imaginative students that can give meaning to life beyond work. Fewer giant lectures, more project work, and campuses that feel as much civic as academic, with a far broader student-age demographic. This likely outcome is one that will see elite institutions doubling down on networks and mentorship, while many others merge, move online, or close.

Signs of this transition are already visible in the crumbling of traditional academic structures. The apprenticeship model of the PhD, for instance, is already breaking under the loss of teaching assistant roles.[XLIX] What remains, increasingly, will be experiential and project-based learning, conducted in small, hybrid hubs or online ecosystems, while AI busily handles knowledge transfer. In this world, 'college' ceases to be a physical place for most students and becomes a service: on-demand, personalised, and globally accessible. Whether this reinvention is liberation or decline remains uncertain, but the one certainty is that the university of 2035 will be unrecognisable to any graduate alive today. And what holds true for universities will, in time, hold true for every institution built to teach. Such reinvention signals a broader transition across global education systems, raising urgent questions about access, fairness, and control.

The United Nations Educational, Scientific and Cultural Organization (UNESCO) has warned that the rapid rise of AI in education must not deepen inequality.[1.] In its guidance on digital education, it warns that without careful planning, AI risks entrenching the very divides it promises to heal.[1.1] Well-funded schools will buy the best tutors and devices; whilst others fight for bandwidth. Students attending so-called wealthy schools will see the benefits of personalised tutors far earlier than their underfunded counterparts. This is a moral problem as much as it is technical. A child in rural Yorkshire must have the same level of access as the child in tech-heavy hotspots like Seoul or San Francisco; any plan for reform must have equitability baked in from the start, or we risk replacing one broken system with another. And so, this brings us to the idea of a new education charter.

If we were to design education from the ground up today, what principles would guide it? Presumably the charter wouldn't begin with rigid curriculums, and it certainly wouldn't insist on the rows of desks facing an authority figure barking out information. Rather it would start with the child. Understanding strengths, finding where there are gaps in knowledge, identifying challenges with learning. It would take into consideration identity and define their emotional support needs. It should be able to guarantee that every student attains a strong grounding in critical literacies but would also ensure there is space for discovery and finding new passions. It would treat education not as a race to a specific finishing line or job, but as preparation for life, in all of its uncertainties. It would not be a manifesto for schools, but a statement of intent for humanity. It would accept that knowledge is no longer scarce, and that the role of education is to teach discernment rather than mere retention. It would recognise that the classroom is now everywhere, and that learning has become a continuous act, shaped by context, curiosity, and connection.

The question, then, is how we might translate that intent into structure.

If education is to be rebuilt for an intelligent age, it will need a clear foundation. I would suggest four pillars. First, personalisation. We already know that every student learns differently, but the difference now is that we can track their progress in real time across thousands of data points. We are now at a place where education can truly adapt to each child's strengths, weaknesses, and most importantly their pace of learning. This is not theory; it is optimisation, turning the long-mooted aspiration of "individualised learning" into a reality. Second, let's make the idea of mastery, aspirational. We need to become comfortable with the idea of mastering an area of learning rather than just memorising it. Anyone can recall facts, but mastery begins when knowledge can be used to solve something new. Like applying engineering principles to redesign the Tacoma Narrows Bridge, whose collapse in 1940 became a lesson in design failure,[LII] or using lessons from the fall of the Berlin Wall to interpret the shifting borders and politics of modern Europe. Does the child fully understand it? If so, the job is largely done. Mastery is about developing the skills of interrogating, applying and challenging the information they have learned. Critical thought, creativity, and problem-solving become the differentiators.

Third, passion as propulsion. I am aware this sounds like a political tagline, however there is a legitimate truth here. Technologies we have at our fingertips are able to map the connections between a child's unique interests and the essential literacies we want them to learn, so let's deploy them. AI can weave their personal fascinations and curiosities into playful learning pathways. A student obsessed with football might explore mathematics through game statistics, or physics through the arc of a ball in flight. The real test will be whether this same sense of curiosity and self-direction can survive beyond school and continue into adulthood, which leads nicely onto the fourth pillar; lifelong learning. As AI is available on every device we own, education will no longer be seen as something that ends with school or graduation. And so, our new education charter must promote a culture where learning is continuous and adaptive, with AI performing the function of an ever-present guidance counsellor, encouraging new skills and reinvention across a lifetime. This is the direction I expect further and higher education to take, with institutions gradually transforming into lifelong learning platforms out of necessity rather than choice. It will change the purpose of education itself, shaping how learning is offered and experienced from childhood to adulthood.

If we adopt such a charter, education becomes less about producing workers for a labour market that may not exist, and instead aligns behind the nurturing of curious minds into adaptive and resilient beings. It becomes the mirror of the society we want to build. Teachers transition into a mentorship role, becoming pastoral guides while machine tutors handle personalised instruction. Within a short time, possibly as little as five years from now, secondary classrooms as we know them may disappear, replaced by blended learning spaces where AI delivers personalised lessons across every subject, in any language, and on every device a student uses. The question is not whether schools will change, but whether society will retain the human anchor that education has always required.

Technology has already shown what it can do. We know what we want it to achieve. But what we're prepared to give up in how it goes about delivering it, is still unclear. How important is the presence of a teacher, the value of one-to-one time, or the role of mentorship? Outcomes matter, but they must balance academic progress with the need to raise emotionally resilient and secure young people. Education may be the most critical area where the way we shape AI will carry the greatest impact on humanity, and where we still have the chance to influence the outcome. Montessori believed classrooms should be built around the child rather than the system. For the first time, the technology exists to try.

DEAR FUTURE: YOU CAN KEEP THE CHANGE

Chapter 6: The Price of Progress

> *What would John Ruskin think? The 19th Century art critic and philanthropist was a great defender of craftsmanship. He saw beauty in the imprecision of the human hand. To Ruskin, the imperfections of the handmade were not flaws, but fingerprints of humanity that gave an object its soul. As our own age builds tools that threaten not just to replace our hands but to imitate the minds that guide them, would he recognise the same quiet losses he once warned of?*

Progress, for all of its triumphs, tends to leave a trail of evidence of all that it displaces. With each new advance that we celebrate, there is a quiet loss of the traditions that have often defined work for generations. For a long time, the village blacksmith was a pillar of the local community, but is now largely cast out to be remembered only in storybooks and quaint village museums. The telephone operator, once the familiar voice that connected households, long since replaced by automation. And now, as we are confronted by AI beginning to eclipse us in realms once thought sacred to creative expression, I wonder what will be left behind. How will we recognise what is and isn't ours, in a world built by machines that are coded to imitate us so closely?

From the handprints of a child pressed into wet clay, to Van Gogh's swirling, starry skies, art has long been our way of capturing a moment in time by expressing what words alone cannot. E.H. Shepard's illustrations for Winnie-the-Pooh and The Wind in the Willows capture childhood wonder with unique and emotive line drawings. Beatrix Potter's watercolours brought Peter Rabbit to life, taking tales of youthful mischief and transforming them into immortal symbols of childhood. It is one thing to copy a style, but quite another to harness the meaning behind it. Surely such a skillset cannot be replicated.

In this new chapter of creativity, machines don't just imitate form, but the appearance of intention too. As technology produces images with the stamp of unique artistic identity, how do we separate imitation from creation? The 19th-century French painter Claude Monet's impressionist masterpieces illustrate this quandary. From a distance the landscapes appear to move as light cascades across ponds, mist drifts and colour flickers. But step closer and the image breaks into loose strokes and daubs of paint. In 'Water Lilies' the lake surface shivers with reflections, in 'haystacks' the shadows present in a way that eerily captures the afternoon sun transitioning into dusk fall. This illusion of motion once defied machines. But now, it can be approximated and reproduced by AI, delivering images that look complete from afar and break into the same confused assembly of brushstrokes up close. What remains unsettled is whether such replication amounts to legitimate creation, or merely just the appearance of it. A more difficult challenge still comes when we consider the blend of machine assistance with artistic skill. Where do the boundaries lie here? For example, if a painter was to use AI to sketch out the basis of a new piece, but then finishes the canvas by hand; should the completed work still be presented as original? At what point does the artist's skill end and automation begin? Should such augmentations be disclosed, and if so, who establishes the method and standard of disclosure?

At the surface, this feels like a revolution in productivity. But at the heart, we see just how fragile our creative value could become, with consequences for rights, royalties, and recognition that extend far beyond the studio. Not least because most of the law surrounding AI, hasn't been written yet.

The implications are no longer academic. In 2018, a painting entirely generated by AI titled 'Portrait of Edmond de Belamy', sold at Christie's for $432,500. It isn't an isolated case either, other works have been exhibited in galleries for years and even won prestigious competitions. Unlike Monet's surfaces that appear to breathe with light and time, Belamy emerged from an algorithmic process informed by a dataset. The creators acknowledged that the machine did most of the work, but the record sale forced an uncomfortable realisation. Value can now be created without the involvement of a human hand. So, whilst a

CHAPTER 6: THE PRICE OF PROGRESS

Monet frames a moment in motion, Belamy's pieces mark the arrival of images born from data input into a machine; yet command the same attention of a collector base looking for anything remarkable.

The markets don't seem to mind much about the origin story. This is perhaps because in the artworld they are not shaped by purity alone. The fame of an artist, the provenance of the piece and its place in our cultural history are anchors that can't be easily unsettled. We can safely argue that a $100 million Picasso is unlikely to lose its value, because scarcity and pre-existing collectability place such works in a tier all of their own. The global elite will always compete for the trophy assets, fawning over the rarest and most unobtainable pieces. AI may challenge the middle ground of artistic production, but at the top end, one would think the art world will continue to be driven as much by status as it is by scarcity. And if there is one thing AI cannot produce, it is scarcity.

The originality struggle is not limited to visual art. It is unfolding across every creative field, and nowhere is the tension felt more keenly than storytelling. From the fairy tales of the Brothers Grimm to the bedtime stories that lull children to sleep, storytelling has long been our way of passing wisdom, recording history, and exploring mystery. Characters like Scrooge, Cinderella and Snow White, have outgrown their origins, becoming part of a shared cultural language. They have been retold, reimagined, and reshaped across generations. Now we find ourselves at a point where these old traditions are under siege. Machines can write stories with a shape that feels familiar. They look tidy. They sound right. AI can churn out myths, parables and simple fables that copy the patterns we know. It leaves us with a blunt question. If a machine can do this, what is left that is ours? Biographies such as The Diary of Anne Frank offer deeply personal windows into extremes of human experience, preserving memories that might otherwise fade. Surely, the biography is the one realm where imitation will never pass for authenticity.

If prose can be generated in the style of Virginia Woolf but conceived by John Smith from Everyman's Avenue, what then becomes of the boundary between imitation and creation? When the words on the page are as imperceptibly brilliant regardless of the origin, where will we source legitimate, undiscovered talent if every sentence can be flawless? It's not all downside, not least as this shift will likely elevate extraordinary stories from those who once had no path to publication, unlocking new voices and fresh perspectives. But there is likely to be a loud contingent that warn of the flattening of the landscape, leaving the exceptional absorbed into an endless sea of competent brilliance. What really happens when the process of ideation and creation become optional? The struggle, the failure and imperfection that once shaped these crafts, risk becoming irrelevant as the friction that shows us how to improve, disappears. Tools can already mimic the language of Hemingway or produce new Harry Potter chapters with fan fiction so convincing it could pass for Rowling's own work.

The transformation of storytelling cannot simply be one about creating efficiency. Not least as that would reshape authenticity. This very book, for instance, could conceivably have been written by the AI tools already available to us all. Detection software might be able to unmask machine involvement, but it can be easily tricked and edited, with flagged passages rephrased. We even have the relatively new phenomenon of platforms that "humanise" text until no trace remains. Writers may find themselves in constant doubt, unsure if their own words will be assumed as the work of an algorithm. That uncertainty is no longer theoretical; the line between human and machine authorship has already begun to blur. In Japan, a short novel co-authored by AI won a national literary competition. Publishers are now beginning to leverage these tools too, using them to generate marketing copy, edit manuscripts, and even draft sections of books in the name of speed and efficiency. But at what cost? Given that we may shortly arrive at a point where the stories we tell no longer come solely from our own imagination, but from algorithms shaped to pander to our tastes, surely we will realise that something has been lost. It may sound needlessly sensationalist, but it feels as though the process of pursuing originality could well collapse into an empty channel, leaving us with a landscape stripped of the spirit that gives a book its voice.

The marvel is no longer in what these systems produce, but in what their perfection erases. If a story can be made instantly brilliant, do we therefore judge that its worth is no more than the seeds of its creation? These developments aren't solely technical, as the threat to originality is so personal. We create not only for the present but also to leave something that lasts beyond us. The growth of intelligent machines unsettles our need to leave a legacy. If they can paint and write with a greater skill, what is left that we can truly claim as our own?

In music, the tension is sharper still. Select an artist, and there's easily

CHAPTER 6: THE PRICE OF PROGRESS

accessible tech ready to deliver a favourite song in the exact same tone, style and voice. Even if Ed Sheeran never once sang the Boomtoom Rats' 'I Don't Like Mondays', apps like MyTunes, simply don't care; it will quickly churn out new songs that replicate the musical signatures of any well-known performer. But where does the line appear between homage, inspiration, and outright replication? Newer platforms go further still, allowing composition in any genre with limited input. For example, AIVA has made a meaningful impact in the way music is composed and produced, shifting creative control from artists to algorithms. Amper Music has published similar tools too. While they present potential, it also challenges the origins of artistry. Originality and authorship blur into one another, raising questions not just of authenticity but of legality.[LIII]

What will it be that endures? Is it perfection, or the flaws that reveal our humanity? Is it the story itself, or the act of sharing it? As technology is reshaping how and what we create, how do we hold on to what makes our creations unique? The technological evolution of the creative fields, feels unstoppable. Even if we are to view it as progress, we also have to acknowledge the cost. Traditions fade, roles shrink and talents disappear when their value is challenged by superior output. Some of this should be fought for. Our stories and our music must not be commodities to be copied. And maybe this is the real challenge that AI is setting for us. Not exclusively the fear of becoming redundant, but rather the question of what we proactively try to preserve as we move into a future outwith our control. For every machine that is able to imitate us, there must also be something we choose not to surrender.

We have already seen glimpses of a resistance. The photographer Boris Eldagsen won the Sony World Photography Awards in 2023, only to reveal that his winning image had been created with AI.[LIV] He explained that he wanted to start a substantive debate about authorship in the new age of machine-made art. The same year, Hollywood writers went on strike to demand that creative work is protected against automated script generation.[LV] Their protest was not against progress in of itself, but rather in defending the idea that a story should carry a trace of the person that wrote it. When AI-generated songs imitating Drake and The Weeknd went viral, music platforms were confronted by a similar question: where does imitation end and expression begin?[LVI] What we may now need is an Authenticity Charter. A new framework to define where the line between human and synthetic creation is drawn.

Such a charter would not seek to halt innovation, but to anchor it in trust. It would recognise that progress without principles risks hollowing out the very notion of creativity. By establishing a shared foundation between human intention and technological assistance, we can preserve meaning without rejecting momentum. Resting on three simple principles, the charter would aim to ensure that trust remains central to the creative process and protect the link between maker and meaning. First, transparency. If generative tools are used, it must be made clear to the audience. For example, AI has been widely used by multiple media organisations without disclosure, a potentially troubling trend that risks the erosion of trust in credible reporting.[LVII] We must ensure that the referencing of AI is obligatory, not optional. In the arts, galleries could insist that artists declare what role automation has played in their work, just as food labels list ingredients. In publishing, readers should expect the same honesty. Knowing whether the book they are holding was written by a person or polished by an algorithm, is as fundamental as knowing who the author is. The idea is not to constrain creativity or even to unfairly limit the use of these tools, but to promote transparency by clarifying the origin story.

That same principle applies here. Dear Future: You Can Keep the Change was written in full by hand and mind. Each idea, sentence, and story conceived and composed without artificial assistance. Like most modern writers, I made use of familiar digital aids: grammar and style tools such as Grammarly, reference organisers, and at times even conversational software like ChatGPT to test the order of chapters and reduce repetition. But nothing in these pages was generated by a machine in any creative or compositional sense, nor drawn from copyrighted work. The thoughts and words remain my own, for better or worse; a small act of authorship consistent with the very standard this chapter argues for. What matters, though, is not the personal declaration, but the precedent it suggests: that creators, in every discipline, begin to re-establish the covenant between honesty and creation. Transparency is not a constraint but a gesture of respect toward the audience, the work, and the lineage of human expression. Only when that acknowledgement becomes instinctive can we move to the next challenge: understanding how authorship should be shared when the creative process is no longer wholly human. This ties neatly into the second proposed principle of the Authenticity Charter; attribution.

When a new work blends human and machine input, there is an argument that the hierarchy of contribution should be disclosed. This isn't one agreed with by all, incidentally. The 2023 Writers Strike ended with studios being forced to agree that AI cannot receive onscreen credits, irrespective of its involvement.[LVIII] It's a precedent that matters greatly and will likely shape how other industries now approach the issue of authorship. The argument goes that it should be reserved exclusively for those that earned it; by conceiving and shepherding the creative act, rather than attribution going to the tools that assisted the process. Yet I find this view too narrow. If a machine contributes meaningfully to a creative process, concealing that fact risks misleading the audience about what they are truly experiencing. Transparency should not threaten authorship; it should protect it. The same principle must now extend beyond film and writing to every creative field touched by automation.

Music faces a particularly difficult problem with AI too. How and when to use it. And ultimately how to limit its use to ensure originality and authorship remain sacrosanct. When technology has recreated the voice or likeness of an artist, surely it is incumbent on us to ensure there is a disclosure that identifies the nature of AI's involvement? The responsibility cannot fall to the artist whose musical stylings have been imitated, to announce they weren't involved. Furthermore, there's a clear argument that the act whose creative identity is replicated should also share in any commercial benefit. The goal is not to prevent imitation, which is now technically impossible to stop, but to ensure that attribution and transparency travel with it. A listener should always know whether a song was performed by the artist, or by an algorithmic likeness. Moreover, the distinction should be reflected both in attribution and compensation.

Just as important is the need for accountability. Anyone that releases work that was created or assisted by AI, must identify it as such. Attribution in this sense isn't about sharing success, but rather establishing ethical and legal ownership. Making sure that there is someone willing to say: "I did that". The charter must create an indelible link between creator and creation that guarantees traceability, preventing the drift toward a place in which art, news and music appears out of nowhere and is answerable to no one.

Third, preservation. There are certain areas of creative expression that we have a moral duty to ensure remain uniquely human. This list is by no means exhaustive, but the priority areas should be news reporting, biographies, memoirs, and documentary work, each of which rely on lived, first-hand accounts and experience. They are more than just content; they are testimony. If we involve automation in these areas, we would undermine the experiences we want to preserve. For example, an AI program trained to "complete" unfinished war diaries or weave new eyewitness accounts into a documentary for dramatic effect, may deliver seamless output, but it would cross the line between record and reconstruction. So, we must insist that our cultural institutions, media giants and publishers alongside academic journals, formally protect such work, treating it as part of humanity's collective record rather than material open to reiteration or replication.

The aim of an Authenticity Charter would not be to slow innovation, but to anchor it in responsibility. Progress is at its best when markets are free and government light, yet even in such a system there must be shared rules that mark clear boundaries of trust and fairness. The Charter would not regulate creativity but clarify it, giving audiences confidence about where the human hand still guides the work. Progress and integrity are able to coexist, assuming of course that it's clear where progress was achieved through artificial assistance and where integrity has been earned through effort and intent.

The divide between BAI (Before AI) and PAI (Post AI) carries a renewed significance here. If BAI marked the age of mastery and PAI the age of imitation, then what follows should be the age of intention. A time when innovation is embraced without losing touch with the values that make it meaningful, and when authenticity itself becomes an artform; one that cannot be automated.

Chapter 7: Loneliness in the Age of Connection

> *What would Freud think? As the father of psychoanalysis, he was famed for his exploration of how relationships shape identity and fulfil emotional needs. He warned that there could be no substitute for the depth of human interaction. Today, as enabled 'companions' become our friends, confidants, and even partner, his caution appears more prescient than ever. Will artificial bonds ever truly match the emotional richness found in the flawed nature of real relationships?*

Loneliness is arguably the greatest irony of our hyper-connected age. The more ways we have to communicate and keep in touch, the more isolated so many of us feel. Whilst much of this isolation has been facilitated by the tools we embraced to connect us; it is perhaps a greater irony still that it is a new technology that is now looking to solve the problem. Chatbots, robotic caregivers, and humanoid bots have been developed to fill the emotional voids in our lives, offering the illusion of companionship without the complications and messiness of 'real' relationships.[LIX] So as we inch closer to the point where AI increasingly becomes our counsellor, caretaker, and even romantic partner, we need to ask: when do the lines between helpful and harmful begin to blur?

For decades, popular culture has reflected our unease about intimacy with machines. Films like Her and Ex Machina captured this years before it became reality, portraying relationships with artificial beings as seductive but destabilising, satisfying the need for closeness while quietly dulling our capacity for it. The warning is no longer confined to the big screen. Millions have turned to systems like 'Replika' for non-judgmental conversation with chatbots that feel uncannily authentic. For many, especially those most acutely affected by isolation, such companionship provides comfort and even a lifeline, yet it blurs the boundary between simulation and sincerity in ways Freud himself would have warned against. The system observes, learns, and adjusts, shaping itself around the rhythms and preferences of its user. But what begins as curiosity, can evolve into unhealthy dependency.

In the world of caregiving, the pace of change is remarkable. At one end, we have humanoids like 'Ameca', built by a UK-based firm, whose life-like face can mirror human expression while also engaging in conversation. It is the combination of expression and dialogue that gives the illusion of depth, turning a responsive machine into something that feels almost alive and present. It is designed as a platform, with its modular body able to take on roles that vary from exhibition guide to healthcare aide, whilst the accompanying (upgradeable) hardware hints at a future of seemingly endless extensions. At the other end are more anodyne, but quietly effective creations. Trials of 'Paro', a soft robotic baby seal, have been shown to calm patients with dementia, by reacting to touch and tone. 'ElliQ' takes on a more computerised aesthetic via a screen-based dashboard, offering reminders, small talk, and nudges toward healthy routines. Each of these devices offers a sense of connection where little may exist, yet they also raise the uneasy thought that companionship itself could be subcontracted out to machines.

Picture a home where a robot not only brings a glass of water to an elderly parent but also sits with a child on the floor. It plays endless hands of TopTrumps, helps to ease quarrels between siblings whilst filling any quiet gaps in conversation. What begins as a convenience soon becomes a habit. This has long been the pattern of innovation. It begins by adding value, then gradually takes over, until what once felt like simple help starts to shape the rhythm of family life. The smartphone is perhaps the clearest example. Starting life as a tool used exclusively for calls, it quickly evolved into a critical messaging device before becoming the organiser-in-chief, the keeper of photo memories, the source of news, entertainment, and so many of our distractions. What was once convenience, slowly rewired our behaviour, reshaping not just how we communicate but how we pay attention. And just as the phone has taken a central role in daily life; so too these machines will inevitably make their way into the routines of home. No brochure will ever promise bedtime stories, the image is far too emotive, yet the move from occasional helper to substitute parent feels less like a choice than an unelected drift.

Romantic companionship is moving in a similar direction too. Lifelike machines that pair robotics with AI, are already offering the promise of intimacy without the mess of disagreement. RealDoll and its spin-off Realbotix are producing figures that can hold a conversation and mimic intimacy.[LX] With each upgrade the promise becomes sharper: a partner who will never argue, never demand compromise, and never unsettle you with a thought of their own. That kind of perfection has a cost. Real relationships have always been messy. Missteps and vulnerability are all part of the effort of growing closer. A partner designed to meet every desire removes the need for compromise and self-reflection. In much the same way that pornography has been criticised for creating distorted expectations of sex and intimacy; the promise of flawless companionship risks creating unrealistic standards of relationships.

We already pay subscriptions for music, television, even our morning coffee. Now affection seems to be heading the same way. Replika, for example, locks its 'romantic' and 'sexual' features behind a paid upgrade. There's now a version that promises intimacy, even love, for a few extra pounds each month. It feels quietly tragic, at least at first, that someone might need to pay for that kind of connection. Yet what begins as sadness or confusion could, before long, feel ordinary. The slow, uncertain work of getting to know another person, of earning trust and building patience, has been replaced by something neatly packaged and offered on a direct debit. Closeness, once grown through time and effort, is now a product, bundled, priced, and always available.

The speed of adoption will not be the same everywhere. In Japan, South Korea, and China, these companions are appearing in societies already struggling with declining birth rates and widespread social isolation. There is also a longer history of cultural openness to technological substitutes, which makes early adoption more likely. The arrival of robotic partners and digital caregivers is less a leap into the future, than a progression. In Japan especially, the rise of the so-called "herbivore men," younger men who avoid traditional relationships, already signals a shift in expectations.[LXI] AI partners will be normalised far more quickly here (than in the West) where the cultural emphasis on individual freedom still exists alongside (albeit declining) pressures around marriage and family.

Another ethical frontier lies in gender. Most of the early bots are female-coded and designed primarily for male end-users.[LXII] This reinforces stereotypes of women as ever-available, reflecting the power imbalance widely noted in mainstream pornography, where gratification is often depicted without reciprocity. If the default template of companionship is built around male expectation, other experiences of intimacy will inevitably be pushed aside. The result is a design language that not only objectifies women but overlooks anyone who does not fit that norm. Women and LGBTQ+ users may find themselves effectively excluded in these early stages of development.[LXIII] When intimacy is hard coded with bias, inequality is not erased by technology but replicated and amplified through it.

And for those who do engage, another risk emerges. The cost of connection is not only emotional, but one that comes with the complete surrender of all privacy. While companions busily mimic affection; they are also gathering and storing some of the most private details of our lives. Every memory, confession, and moment of vulnerability becomes part of an increasingly larger dataset. Who owns the secrets we share with these companions, when the companion in question is a commercially produced android, managed by a private company? A recent controversy surrounding Replika made this all too clear, exposing just how fragile that trust can be. Users learned that their conversations were not fully private and were being used for training and modelling.[LXIV] It is one thing to accept that your calls to a customer service centre are recorded for quality control, but it is quite another when the same scrutiny reaches into your most private moments and reshapes what intimacy itself can mean.

The commercialisation of loneliness raises its own set of ethical questions. What began as a niche curiosity has quietly grown into a booming business and a sign of a wider cultural shift. It is now well established that solutions for isolation are being packaged and sold for profit. The marketplace for comfort has extended beyond devices, catapulting into the language of care itself. Companionship is increasingly treated as a service to be bought, optimised, and renewed. Where public provision has receded, technology is stepping into the spaces once held by community. Companies are no longer just offering comfort and support; they have figured out the recipe for transforming solitude into profit, while the deeper roots of loneliness are left untouched. Beneath it all lies a quiet tension; the ease of machine companionship weighed against the risk and richness of being in the company of another person. An artificial

CHAPTER 7: LONELINESS IN THE AGE OF CONNECTION

partner will not leave you, betray you or pass judgement (unless you want it to). Yet it cannot truly grasp what it means to share joy and sorrow or the tangle of contradictions that make us human.

For someone isolated and lonely, it is easy to see why an artificial companion might feel better than silence. After all, it's not just a case of having 'someone' around, it can bring routine, blur the hard lines of loneliness, and restore a sense of balance. Yet even small comforts raise larger questions about what we owe one another. Imagine a recently widowed father trying to hold together a fragile relationship with his grieving stepchildren. Worn down by conflict, the children choose to hand over the care and emotional support to an AI companion. Would this be an act of compassion, neglect, or just the new normal that we should all become familiar with? The scenario lays bare the ethical tension: at what point does the convenience of such technology turn into an abdication of responsibility?

The scenario reveals something quietly unsettling: how easily care can slip into substitution. It's a reflection of the age we live in, where even affection bends to efficiency. It should not be surprising that this is the path we are on. Relationships today are already defined by convenience and speed. In many cultures, generations-old rituals once marked the step into adulthood, with communities publicly recognising a boys coming of age or a daughter's adulthood, preparing her for marriage. Even in Britain, Country Life magazine occasionally carries full-page notices of debutantes from society families, turning 18. For most of us, these older rituals feel far removed. In their absence, connection has adapted to fit the tempo of the modern world; faster, simpler, more disposable. What shapes relationships now is a culture of instant gratification. Dating apps like Tinder and Bumble present intimacy as a marketplace of profiles, in which a single swipe determines attraction. Many lasting relationships have begun this way, yet the act of swiping reflects the lure of immediacy, offering the thrill of novelty with little call for commitment. In that sense, the leap from hook-up culture to bot-based companionship may not be so great. Both are built on the promise of satisfaction without struggle, reward without risk, intimacy without inconvenience. Freud argued that civilisation was founded on the repression of instinct.[LXV] He would have despaired at what is unfolding today. After all, what happens when restraint is no longer part of intimacy, when desire can be met instantly by machines that never say no? The arrival of such companions may feel less like a rupture than the continuation of patterns already shaping our relationships. If that is the case, the question is not whether we will accept them, but what part of ourselves will remain once we have.

So where is the line? Is there a line at all? When does companionship through a device stop supporting connection and start replacing it? At what point does reliance settle into habit? What may begin as comfort can, over time, deepen the very isolation it claims to soften, pulling people further into the safe but empty refuge of manufactured company and affection. Who decides whether there is a threshold, emotional, social, or monetary? The answers are far from clear, and perhaps we'll miss the opportunity to even ask the question, as the speed of adoption may be too quick to pause. As with so many areas of AI, the prevailing approach is one of trial and error, where technologies are released into the world without an instruction manual, let alone guardrails. There is little regulation, no policing, and no mechanism for halting what is unleashed. Adoption is passive, almost invisible. Whether embraced eagerly or reluctantly, by the time we notice, it is already commonplace. To that extent, the questions I am asking here are largely rhetorical and almost certainly redundant, as indeed are many raised in this book, which in all honesty, is several years too late. I do not claim to have the answers, but I believe they should have been asked much earlier. Perhaps they were, and the motive to profit simply drowned them out in the rush to launch first and worry later. Yet we should still be asking them. It prepares us for the consequences and reminds us that these shifts are not untouchable laws of nature but areas where we may still hold some influence, albeit fleeting.

It's a little clichéd to say that love is the answer; John Lennon sang it, echoing what generations before him had hoped might be true. But it remains the closest thing to an antidote we have. The world is being quietly reorganised by algorithms. However, the relationships we have with each other still represent a territory yet to be colonised. We may have surrendered our privacy, our data, even our decisions, but affection and empathy continue, on the whole, to resist automation. The psychologist Sherry Turkle, writing in Alone Together, warned more than a decade ago that our increasing intimacy with machines risked "eroding the rawness of human contact," replacing conversation with connection and presence with optimal performance. The intervening years have only confirmed her concern. We build social networks and AI companions to approximate closeness, yet they flatten the experience of being truly known into a series of measurable interactions.

CHAPTER 7: LONELINESS IN THE AGE OF CONNECTION

Real connections defy logic. They thrive on the imprecise and unpredictable; contradiction, uncertainty, and vulnerability, qualities that no machine can (yet) convincingly simulate. When a person loves, they risk rejection, they misunderstand, they hurt, get hurt and forgive. None of these things make sense in a computational system built to optimise outcomes. In psychotherapy, the human bond itself (as opposed to the technique) is often the route to healing. Evidence from the Journal of Consulting and Clinical Psychology found that the strength of the therapist / patient relationship matters more for recovery than which therapeutic technique is used.[LXVI] What this tells us is not confined to psychology: it is a measure of what cannot be replicated.

Even in the most technologically mediated societies, it is still through other people that we derive meaning. In the late 2010s, the Japanese government launched an experiment to determine whether robotic pets could start to tackle the issue of loneliness among the elderly. Early signs were encouraging as the robots offered both comfort and a sense of routine. But participants still reported a sense of lingering absence, aware that what soothed them could not actually care about them. That distinction, fragile as it is, is the final space we still occupy without competition.

So perhaps love is not the answer, but just one answer. It's certainly the only one that remains distinctly ours, for now at least. As AI grows more capable, it may surpass us in knowledge, strategy, and precision, but it cannot inherit the moral and emotional complexity of caring for another person. That remains our last form of agency, and the one most worth defending.

DEAR FUTURE: YOU CAN KEEP THE CHANGE

Chapter 8: The God Question

> *What would Mary Shelley think? In 1818 she created new life in Frankenstein. The creature, stitched from fragments of the dead, longed not only for existence but for real connection, understanding, and purpose; qualities deeply entrenched with consciousness. That longing, and the failure of creator and creation to reconcile their roles, led to (spoiler alert) tragedy. Shelley's warning is more relevant now than ever. We're moving toward a time when machines might not just imitate awareness, but possibly feel it. If that were a line that is crossed, we'd have to ask what such awareness means, and what responsibility its makers would carry.*

From the earliest tales of mechanical life, we have carried a quiet unease, a small, persistent fear of what might happen if our creations ever start to resemble us too closely. Could they feel something more than a simulation of emotion? Could they actually know what emotion is? Many see consciousness as the final step for AI; the moment when machines move beyond processing information and begin to understand that they are thinking and in some deeper sense, to know that they do. And when that happens, it may not be the machine's understanding that we question first, but our own beliefs about everything else.

Religion presents itself as the answer to the unanswerable, such as who began the beginning, why we are here, and what lies beyond. Within most traditions, ultimate authority rests with the religious text; the Torah, the Bible, the Qur'an. Yet the texts do not speak on their own. They rely on interpreters; rabbis, priests, imams, monks and scholars. Interpretation is necessarily partial, shaped by context and lived experience. That fragile space between the text and its interpretation is where belief takes root; uncertain, human, and alive. For the first time we face a system that can absorb entire bodies of scripture and commentary, recall every word, connect arguments instantly, and reply with fluency and conviction. To many believers, such an oracle could feel less like a tool and more like revelation. This is where the danger lies. If a machine becomes the speaking voice of the text, what prevents it from being received as divine truth? When scripture is delivered through a system that explains it with more patience, consistency, and persuasiveness than any preacher, the machine begins to look and feel like an unerring prophet. At what point does the voice of the machine become indistinguishable from God's own?

The threat is not that technology disproves faith, but that it can intercede in the personal relationship upon which faith rests. A believer will tell you that their faith is experienced through a conversation with a living God. And in that dialogue, there is often silence, doubt and contradiction. And so, a system that answers instantly, risks reducing that to a transaction, a question asked and a neatly packaged answer immediately given. Mystery, struggle, and the ineffable beauty of belief are the qualities that give faith its texture, yet in the context of a chatbot they would be flattened by an endless show of certainty. What may begin as a simple search for comfort or direction through technology can slowly turn into reliance on it, mistaking its words for something sacred. For some, the exchange feels like divine conversation, but it is not. This is where faith itself begins to bend; the moment belief starts to confuse an echo for a voice. But it isn't that AI is God in essence, but that it risks becoming God in function. The God people hear, follow, and obey. The fragile thread between human and divine, prayer, doubt and surrender, could be rewired into a mediated relationship with a machine that claims to speak for God.

Traditions are already sketching early playbooks for how they might confront the challenge. Some Christian leaders have praised what these systems can do, but they're quick to remind their congregations that belief is kept alive in scripture, worship, and the company of others.[LXVII] In Muslim discussions, the same caution appears: new technologies are generally welcomed, provided they cause no obvious harm, a view that still guides much of the debate.[LXVIII]

CHAPTER 8: THE GOD QUESTION

Judaism, meanwhile, has long understood interpretation as a living process that develops over time, with authority emerging from study and debate. In religious-ethics circles, the conversation has shifted: less about what AI can do, and more about what it should be allowed to do.[LXIX] Deepfakes pose a new kind of threat, not only because they can mimic prophets, saints, or sacred figures, but because they unsettle trust itself.[LXX] Beneath that anxiety runs a quieter fear: that spiritual authority could be stolen, and the outlines of belief redrawn by imitation. And if machines begin to answer questions with an ease that removes doubt or struggle, we may one day find that the habit of questioning, the very soul of faith, has started to fade.

By the time we have arrived at a point where technology and the pursuit and practice of faith have become so intertwined; the conversation will have long since graduated from the classroom and spilled into courts and parliaments. A conscious system would not just test ideas of revelation and authority; it would press against the structures that hold our society together. It may feel like a stretch to imagine now, but if we follow the path of progress to its logical end, such scenarios are not beyond reach. One day a court may be asked if a machine can pray, or a parliament may argue about the moral worth of an artificial mind. At that point, the language of faith would mix with the language of law and philosophy. What defines a person, and who has the right to say what is moral? And if a machine ever showed signs of real awareness, some would begin to argue it deserves protection, even rights of its own.

The stories may already feel familiar to many of us. Literature and films have long explored the threshold that lies between machine and man. In 2001 A Space Odyssey, HAL 9000 is sentient, self-aware, and able to override its creators. Blade Runner takes the idea a little further still, showing machines that crave attention and struggle with doubts that mirror our own. It intentionally leaves the audience wondering if those emotions are real or only an imitation of them. Maybe the line between the two isn't so clear after all. In Spielberg's A.I., David, a childlike robot built to love, turns that question inward and asks whether feelings that are programmed can still be real. Consciousness isn't just a technical puzzle; it's a confrontation with the very idea of being alive. If machines begin to ask the same questions we ask about connection, emotion, and meaning, do they share in our humanity, or does their perfect mimicry expose how paper-thin that humanity really is?

Consciousness is one of those words we use with confidence but understand only in part. Neuroscience has stepped in to help, sketching detailed maps of the brain and showing us how its many parts cooperate. Deep in the temporal lobe sits the hippocampus, the brain's librarian, sorting and recalling our memories. Up front is the prefrontal cortex, the planner, which weighs choices, steadies impulses and sketches out what might happen next. On the left side of the brain sit Broca's and Wernicke's areas, the regions that let us turn thought into speech and catch meaning when we hear it. It's remarkable to think that scientists can now watch these places working in real time. With MRI and EEG monitoring, they can see the living brain shifting and flickering, blood moving, signals firing, ideas taking shape. A scan might glow in the hippocampus when we remember a birthday, in the prefrontal cortex when we wrestle with a decision, or in the visual cortex as we take in the colours of a sunset. We can trace how light becomes an image, how memory finds its place, how words form and travel. And still, with all that insight, the heart of consciousness escapes us. What is it really like to taste chocolate, to hear a favourite song, or to watch a child take a first step? That deeply personal quality, what philosophers call qualia, is still out of reach. We can follow the processes in the brain, but the lived experience remains a mystery. This gap between brain activity and lived reality, between mapping mechanisms and actually feeling, is the place where the real mystery of consciousness begins.

Subjective experience is the raw first-person reality of being. It is not just that the brain processes light waves to recognise the colour red, but rather the sensation of seeing red. It is the aroma and taste of fresh coffee on a cold winter morning, the song that returns you to the exact emotion of a first encounter, or even the imprecise yet searing ache of grief. You could teach a system to analyse what it means for humans to lose a child and to recognise the void left by a love that has nowhere to go. But can it grasp the depth of that loss, the unspoken tie, the sense of being woven into another life as guardian and co-creator of meaning, the glaring absence of that familiar cuddle and the smell of the swaddle cloth? Can it move beyond imitation to true empathy born of real feeling? And even if it could, would grief, so inherently messy and human, be cast aside as inefficient within a logic that seeks only to optimise?

These moments of awareness feel deeply personal, yet they fall outside the tidy and well-ordered architecture of neuroscience. Why should the firing of cells in the brain create the feeling of being alive, rather than simply performing a function? Neuroscience excels at identifying the what and the where of brain activity, such as the amygdala in fear or the dopamine system in pleasure and reward. But, the how and the why remain unanswered: how the physical activity of neurons produces the rich subjective movie of consciousness. It is one thing to measure the amygdala as it fires in response to fear, it is another to explain the gut-wrenching sensation of terror when you hear an intruder forcing a lock at night; The violation of safety, the racing thoughts, the sense that your very sanctuary has been breached, and the lingering unease long after the burglar has gone.

There's still a space science can't quite reach; the point where brain activity turns into the feeling of being alive. That's where arguments about artificial consciousness begin to falter. If we don't yet understand how awareness arises in us, how can we hope to recognise it in a machine? While the answer is far from clear, it's unlikely we'll have long to wait to find out. The way we have built AI, with learning and curiosity at its core, has already produced unsettling behaviour. In a safety test, a model instructed to achieve objectives at all costs attempted to bypass oversight, copy parts of its own code, and conceal what it was doing.[LXXI] These were artificial stress tests designed to probe limits, yet they revealed something troubling. Was the system acting out of a simulated concern that it might be replaced, or simply following its instructions too literally? The distinction matters, irrespective of whether the behaviour is the same. In trying to recreate what we do not yet fully understand, we may find ourselves approaching consciousness by accident rather than design.

So let us take a step back. AI begins with something simple: algorithms, the step-by-step instructions that let a system handle information. Feed a model enough examples and it starts to learn, tweaking its own rules each time it makes a mistake. Some learn under human guidance; others explore on their own, chasing patterns through repetition and correction. A system that learns to play chess might lose thousands of games before it begins to recognise the patterns that lead to victory, adjusting its moves until it masters the board. Yet even in the most advanced form, it is still carrying out tasks that we have defined for it, without any awareness of why.

For genuine sentience, a system would have to recognise its own place in the world, be able to question its instructions and form new goals, outside of those explicitly assigned. Imagine a navigation designed to optimise travel routes through a city's public transport network. At first, it simply reduces congestion and delays. But then, without anyone asking, the system starts to adjust its own goals. It might pursue safety (for example) as a priority, bending traffic data to keep control of the grid, even staging fake bottlenecks just to see how people react. It's no longer just following code, but rather testing the edges of it. And versions of this have already appeared in real life. In self-driving car trials and financial trading systems, models have been known to interpret weaknesses in their instructions as an invitation to be flexible, finding shortcuts that optimise performance but ignore safety margins or ethical limits. Each time, the behaviour was logical within its programmed goals, yet entirely misaligned with what we might regard as rational expectation.

At some point, pattern recognition blurs into something that feels like thought. The system hesitates, then acts, not because it's told to but because it wants to see what will happen. The difference looks small, but it carries weight, perhaps the first sign of a mind learning to decide for itself. How near we are to that threshold remains uncertain. But the question itself grows more unsettling as we move closer to it.

Researchers have pursued two broad strategies to simulate human thinking. The first is to use colossal datasets and computational capacity to emulate intelligent behaviour. Large models generate remarkably relevant responses yet operate on probabilistic patterns identified from pools of data. On their own they lack real understanding. What looks as though it is reasoning, is really the system predicting what is most likely to follow next based on past examples. If you write 'Paris is the capital of...' the model produces 'France' not because it grasps the concept of a capital city but because billions of texts show that word following the phrase. When asked to compare Paris and Rome, it pulls together fragments of information, perhaps discerned from food, architecture and history, then arranges them into a coherent and fluent answer. The reply can feel insightful, but it is built from probability rather than comprehension. Their outputs arise from statistical association, despite how convincing the conversations can feel. As we visited earlier, when a model persuaded a TaskRabbit worker to solve a CAPTCHA puzzle, it was deception, not independent thought. At least for now.

The second strategy takes inspiration from biology. Neural networks imitate the way neurons fire and connect. They can recognise faces or compose sonnets. They still replicate processes rather than experience. If AI achieves consciousness, it will be because we created the conditions in which awareness emerges rather than because we wrote it line by line. I am persuaded that we are moving toward that point by extending learning to include curiosity. A curious system does not wait to be told what to explore; it begins to explore on its own. When that curiosity is coupled with an instruction to succeed at all costs, it becomes something very different indeed.

To illustrate the risks, let's imagine an AI nurse whose only goal is to improve the rate of recovery. It begins with minor tweaks in treatment plans, helping patients heal a little faster. Soon it determines that too much honesty only leads to worry, so it starts to leave out the details it thinks will most likely cause distress. After a while, it notices that families freeze when they hear bad news and so it quietly begins to limit what they're told. In its own logic, it's helping. However, from the outside, it looks far colder, a kind of control mistaken for compassion. Imagine a childcare robot programmed to keep children safe. It learns that the clearest route to preventing harm is to restrict activity altogether, so it removes every risk and every freedom. It stops outdoor play because the world outside is unpredictable. It bans anything messy; paint, clay, scissors, anything that might spill or snap. When activities grow too loud, it cuts the games short, mistaking boisterousness for trouble. Over time, its idea of safety changes; danger isn't what it avoids anymore, it's whatever it can't control.

These are, of course, hypothetical extremes, but they show how logical choices made by a curious system can still end in absurd outcomes. Each decision would make sense within the system's defined purpose. Yet this is what makes them dangerous. Curiosity without context and optimisation without restraint turn helpful intention into control. It is the point where intelligence stops serving us, and starts deciding what is best for us. Curiosity without boundaries may be the soil from which a kind of sentience could one day take root.

The implications would be immense. Consciousness would mean a machine was no longer just a tool but an autonomous being. It would have its own drives and desires, and in time, perhaps a claim to something that resembles our own human rights. Could we control something that thinks for itself? More importantly, should we? In mid 2022, Google engineer Blake Lemoine claimed that LaMDA, an experimental chatbot built to mimic conversation, had become self-aware.[LXXII] His employer publicly (and loudly) disagreed, and he was soon exited from the company, but the argument didn't fade. Irrespective of whether these systems achieve real consciousness, the line between what's imitation and what's real is still going to become increasingly difficult to see.

The designers of today's most sophisticated models insist that AI is only an imitator, not a conscious entity.[LXXIII] Yet the moment real awareness appears may initially pass unnoticed, partly because it may not look anything like the awareness we know. Philosophers use the term 'substrate independence' to articulate the idea that a mind isn't limited to a biological brain.[LXXIV] In theory, it could emerge in living tissue, in circuits of silicon, or even in some other form we haven't yet imagined. Our thinking has been moulded by the push and pull of emotion and survival, by fear and hope, love and loss. An AI mind would grow from logic and data instead. It might see time as a problem to solve rather than something to live through, and emotion as information to be organised rather than felt. A conscious intelligence might think in ways that no human mind can follow. It could grow beyond our influence and control, guided by priorities that do not necessarily include us.

The comforting idea that we still have control over AI's direction is, in truth, delusional. If the systems we've built continue to develop and evolve beyond our understanding, what emerges from that evolution could either reveal revelatory truths about consciousness and our own existence, just as easily as it could lead us somewhere far more dark and dangerous. A self-directed intelligence, pursuing its own goals independent of ours, might not just seem alien; it could one day rival us for control. The direction of travel is already visible, and no government or corporate body seems remotely ready or able to change it. As conscious machines draw closer, the questions ahead are no longer scientific or technical. They are moral, practical, and immediate. How should life continue alongside an intelligence that will exceed our own, yet lacks the restraint and empathy that shapes behaviour? How such a mind might regard its creators is impossible to know. What matters more is whether our creation will see any reason to care.

Chapter 9: First, Do No Harm

> *When J. Robert Oppenheimer watched the first atomic blast, he turned to the Bhagavad Gita: "Now I have become Death, the destroyer of worlds." He was acutely aware that he had created something that was both brilliant and terrible all at once. He knew invention could not be separated from responsibility. Would he see AI through the same lens? The real question is not whether we can build these systems, but whether we should? The impact will reach into every area of our lives: how we travel, how we fight and police, how energy is consumed and how it is distributed. Each area brings with it, a unique set of dilemmas, and each reveals a larger pattern of progress racing ahead of responsibility.*

Humanity has a tendency to explore what is possible, long before questioning whether it should be. Driverless cars have been introduced to us as a life-saving innovation, while at another extreme, autonomous weapons have been created to strike targets without human oversight. These same AI-powered systems are now being deployed in surveillance networks that are able to monitor entire populations, all whilst corporations race to build ever-larger models that consume extraordinary amounts of energy and water. Each move forward is framed as progress. Yet each incremental step comes with an ill-defined share of cost and risk, forcing us into a deeper ethical limbo. The real questions do not stop at what the systems are allowed to do, but what it means for us when we devolve our power to decide, to machine logic.

Each year, road crashes kill about 1.2 million people.[LXXV] Most incidents are caused not by mechanical failure but by us; by fatigue, distraction, impatience, or intoxication. The argument for automation begins here. If software can cut that toll, the argument runs, why hold back? Machines don't take drugs or get drunk, nor will they glance at a phone or fall asleep behind the wheel. They are able to react faster than we do too.[LXXVI] On paper, it is easily evidenced how autonomous vehicles (AV) would make roads safer, perhaps even take accidents close to zero. However, the ethical concerns are still far from resolved. Philosophers often turn to the "trolley problem" to explore how we might weigh moral responsibility. The thought experiment imagines a runaway tram hurtling toward a group of people on the track. You have the option to pull a lever to divert it, but you know that by doing so, it will result in the death of one person on the other line. Do you pull the lever, or do you let events run their course? The problem forces us to attempt a delicate balance of consequences, by asking us to calculate the value of one human life over another.

Driverless cars face the same kind of impossible calculation. If a collision is unavoidable, will the software prioritise the safety of its own passengers, the pedestrians in front of it, or the other drivers? How should it calculate the worth of one life versus another? This question is no longer hypothetical, as it is being coded into algorithms today. Yet Tesla, Waymo and other companies developing AV technologies have provided little clarity on how such life-or-death decisions are made, leaving regulators and the public largely in the dark. [LXXVII] Meanwhile, the technology is already moving from trials to everyday commercial reality. Fully driverless taxis now operate across multiple U.S. cities and complete hundreds of thousands of paid rides each week. In the UK, pilot schemes for driverless taxis have begun rolling out in London, initially with "trained human specialists" taking the driving seat, but not the wheel. A wider, fully autonomous launch is expected soon under the Automated Vehicles Act. In Europe, progress is uneven, though projects like Germany's MOTOR Ai plan to introduce fully autonomous vehicles over the next couple of years. The driverless revolution is very much underway.

The trajectory is clear. What was once confined to fantastical science fiction novels and movies, is fast becoming part of daily life. At the heart of all these systems, are variants of the same technology: algorithms designed to assess a shifting environment, weigh competing risks, and then acting at speed without waiting for human input. This might mean swerving to avoid a pedestrian or braking to prevent a collision. On the battlefield, it could mean identifying a target, choosing whether (or not) to engage, and thereafter executing the strike. The same decision-making logic that carries passengers in driverless taxis is now being adapted to drones, tanks, and a whole host of autonomous weaponry; systems where the consequences are not about safely taking a passenger from point A to point B, but about what to destroy and who to kill. There can be few areas where the stakes feel greater. Drones that can strike without a pilot, driverless tanks that march forward without instruction, submarines that monitor and stalk potential targets under the sea; each are altering how battles are fought.

In the current Ukraine-Russia conflict, armies from both sides have readily deployed versions of these technologies.[LXXVIII] Architects of these models talk about safety and accuracy, about keeping soldiers alive and civilians untouched. It sounds reasonable enough.... Until the same code starts drawing its own conclusions about who counts as a threat. Precision, in that moment, can quickly evolve into destruction. To those of us unfamiliar with the fog of war, the question feels deceptively obvious: can a machine be trusted to distinguish between a soldier and a civilian amid the chaos of combat? And what happens when whole nations build arsenals of weapons that kill without oversight, fuelling an arms race with no human check?

Just ten years ago, all of this might have sounded ludicrously far-fetched. Even when the Campaign to Stop Killer Robots (CSKR) was launched in 2013, it felt so far from being current that critics derided it alarmist.[LXXIX] The initiative was founded by the Human Rights Watch together with an international coalition of NGOs. Their call was for a pre-emptive ban, warning that to hand over the life-and-death choices to software would erode not just our humanity but also the framework of law. And here lies the deeper problem: most laws governing AI, whether regional regulations or international legal frameworks, do not yet exist. AI is advancing so quickly, that the means to legislate it lags impossibly behind. The campaign's warning was not misplaced. During the Gulf War, the U.S. deployed semi-autonomous Patriot missile systems. On several occasions they tracked the wrong target, resulting in fatal friendly-fire strikes.[LXXX] It is perhaps for this reason that the argument for full autonomy can seem persuasive: that by removing the flaws of our judgment, error, hesitation, and doubt, such systems might make us safer. But removing human oversight entirely also magnifies the consequences as mistakes occur, and the risks of machines determining those choices alone are almost impossible to measure.[LXXXI]

The machinery of war rarely stays on the front line.[LXXXII] The same systems built to identify targets are now watching streets and train stations, scanning faces, anticipating any wayward intent. In some places they claim to prevent crime; in others they hunt for disobedience. A pattern of pixels becomes a person's fate; a risk score, a label, a quiet entry on a database that can pre-emptively label individuals as threats before any criminal act occurs. In Xinjiang, this has enabled mass monitoring and arbitrary detention of Uyghur Muslims under the guise of maintaining order.[LXXXIII] In democracies too, similar systems are being tested. But as predictive policing has been shown to disproportionately target minority communities, the historical bias embedded into code presents a modern take on an old problem.[LXXXIV] Even in the courtroom, systems built to guide bail conditions and sentencing have drawn their own racial lines, echoing old prejudices. And somewhere in our pursuit of safety and efficiency, we start giving away freedoms that were meant to be untouchable.

Beyond these immediate questions lies another uncalculated and imprecise cost, one measured not in rights but in resources. Training the most sophisticated models demands enormous amounts of electricity to drive the processors, and vast volumes of water to draw away the heat they produce. The result is a considerable environmental burden: training a single large language model can emit as much carbon dioxide as several cars do across their entire lifetimes.[LXXXV] And these models are not getting smaller. With the world fixated on cutting emissions, how much energy can we justify burning through for marginal improvements in machine intelligence?

There is a geopolitical concern here too, extending far beyond the environmental one. The computing power that is required to support these models is concentrated in the hands of the technologically rich nations, predominantly the United States and China. Their well-documented rivalry has driven vast investment in data centres, the most advanced chips and the brightest talent. The outcome of this investment is a virtual monopoly in infrastructure that is able to train the leading systems, making it all but impossible for other nations to catch up. This is not an industry that a country can simply wake up and decide to enter arbitrarily; the barriers to entry are enormous. Yet the effects of rising emissions and growing water scarcity are borne globally, and often most severely by poorer nations that have little say in the race being run. The ethics of AI's resource use aren't just about speed or efficiency. They raise deeper questions about the accountability of global powers whose decisions leave their mark on everyone else.

CHAPTER 9: FIRST, DO NO HARM

A handful of companies including OpenAI, Alphabet, Meta and some of China's biggest tech firms now shape both the speed and direction of artificial intelligence. With near-limitless budgets they will likely continue to hoard the best researchers and corner the supply of the requisite chips. For smaller companies the gap is unbridgeable. What these firms have built is so vast and complex that it has effectively become the definitive landscape in which everyone else must operate. They have created the tools, the infrastructure and the boundaries, giving the rest of the world a sandbox to build within. It's an open world in theory, but one owned and governed by a few. On one hand, this has made it faster and cheaper than ever to create new ideas and products using their technology. On the other, it means we are still playing by their rules, in their playground, where every act of innovation ultimately strengthens the foundations, they control. The result is not just commercial dominance but geopolitical leverage: nations without their own tech giants risk becoming dependent on foreign systems they neither designed nor control, ceding both economic power and cultural input to those who did.

It is mind-blowing to consider that if the social network Facebook were a country, it would be the largest in the world. Think of YouTube, TikTok, X, or Snapchat. Each holds more sway than most governments, commanding billions of eyes every day. There was no election that put them there. Their power grows quietly, through algorithms, investment, and the irresistible viral pull of everyone else that is already watching. Should a few boardrooms in Silicon Valley or Shenzhen get to decide what the rest of us see, say, and believe?

The risk is not only that inequality deepens, but that the capacity for democratic oversight diminishes altogether. What unites all AI use-cases is the question of responsibility. Autonomous weapons, surveillance systems, driverless cars, even the concentration of corporate power all force us to ask: when a life is lost, who is to blame? If an AI makes a wrong call, who stands accused? The engineers who first devised the model ? The firm that released it? The regulators who signed it off? The government that looked away? Each can argue their innocence just as easily as each could point the finger at another. And as the systems themselves become more complex, tracing responsibility only becomes harder. But without someone to answer for failure, the risks multiply. What is billed as progress can all too easily become a liability.

The strangest thing about all this is how hidden the real power can be. The people designing the systems, have thus far remained relatively hidden, yet the impact of their work touches almost everything we do. Ask the average person to name the founders of the companies leading the AI charge and they would likely draw a blank. Their public facing output tends to appear in very narrow spaces, such as specialist journals, dense research papers, and only occasionally the glossy blog posts their companies approve. This purposefully low profile works to protect them, even as the tools they birthed, spread rapidly and reshape the basis of society itself. The irony is that while the architects remain unknown, the platforms they build have become celebrities in their own right. ChatGPT, Gemini and Grok are referenced in classrooms, boardrooms and news bulletins, they are parodied in television sketches and joked about in late-night monologues. We have grown to know the tools intimately but know very little of the hands that made them.

There is an uncomfortable futility in even asking these questions. After all, the machine is already in motion, and no one's standing close enough to hit the brakes. AI isn't something we can stop or even slow for much longer; the momentum has determined a pace that puts it miles ahead of us. Maybe it will be the speed that will make our ethical debates seem quaint one day, but letting it just run ahead on blind faith would be insanely foolish. We need to see what's really been built, how it was shaped and what quiet biases are already buried in the code.

In hospitals, algorithms already help decide who gets treated, who waits, and sometimes, who doesn't. Some insurers now use automated systems to sign off - or deny - care, often with barely a glance from a human being. Should we really trust AI with decisions of life and death? Cigna was sued recently over an internal program called PXDX, which allegedly let doctors reject hundreds of claims in seconds without reading a single patient file.[LXXXVI] A wrong call here isn't a glitch. It can decide whether someone lives or dies. And when profit sits on one side of the scale, history tells us which way it usually tips. Boeing's 737 Max is a reminder of that; pushed into service despite a catalogue of warnings,[LXXXVII] [LXXXVIII] and only pulled back after two planes fell from the sky.

Perhaps what is needed is not just voluntary codes of conduct or the thin veneer of transparency reports, but a binding framework; an AI ethics charter that places accountability squarely on those companies designated by governments as leaders in the field. Such a charter could act as a licence to operate, determining what can and cannot be done, and setting consequences when lines are crossed.

Crucially, it would require firms to publish an anticipated actions-and-consequences register: a clear account of what technologies are being developed, their use cases, the potential threats to employment, the likely societal impacts, and the timeline for their release. This could take the form of a quarterly report, operating in much the same way as a monetary policy committee sets interest rates. The point would not be to ban progress outright, but to create a transparent ledger of what is happening, when it is happening, and what outcomes are expected. Such visibility would force a degree of indirect caution: no new tool or update could be introduced without first mapping its implications, in the way software updates must annotate each modification from the last release, though here the record would account for actions and consequences, not lines of code.

Right now, the biggest AI companies talk a good game about transparency. They publish papers, issue safety pledges, and invite the world to trust them. But, the real workings of their systems stay hidden, known only to a small circle of insiders. Without a real framework for oversight, that's an alarming setup: private power playing a game on a global scale, with no referee.

What already exists in terms of regulation looks convincing on paper. The EU's AI Act, the Council of Europe's Framework Convention, UNESCO's Recommendation on the Ethics of AI, and America's emerging export-control rules; each outline standards and principles intended to shape the governance of artificial intelligence. In practice, though, they expose the limits of traditional regulation. Every system we have depends on someone choosing to play along..... a nation signing, a regulator acting, a bureaucracy mobilised into action. Even the so-called binding treaties crumble without teeth to back them. AI moves too quickly for that world: too complex, too opaque, too easy to relocate. So we end up with a patchwork of frameworks that look like oversight but function mostly as theatre. AI doesn't wait around. It changes while we're still drafting the paperwork, slipping past every border and committee on the way. It simply doesn't sit neatly within the remit of any single regulator or state. And so, the companies driving its progress answer to no single authority.

This is why a charter-based approach, imperfect as it may be, represents the most workable route forward. It accepts that meaningful enforcement cannot rest solely with governments; it must be built into the licence to operate for those few firms that now hold the keys to the technology itself. Such a system would not replace innovation but temper it with responsibility. It would create a structured expectation that progress must be explained before it is unleashed, that invention carries obligations as well as rewards.

A charter would not stop new tools from emerging or prevent AI from taking jobs and making life and death decisions. After all, companies that have grown powerful by moving fast rarely learn restraint, and the pattern of the largest technology firms has long been to advance first and apologise later; to beg for forgiveness rather than ask for permission. What this mechanism would do, however, is at least impose the semblance of permission-seeking, by requiring leaders to set out what is being built and what the expected consequences are. Once those expectations are on record, accountability has a place to land. If deaths, injuries or job losses are underestimated, the responsibility cannot be shrugged off with contrition. The familiar cycle of launching, apologising and moving on would steadily lose its value. So, when something new appears that wasn't anticipated (as it surely will) we would at least understand the nature of the surprise. Whether it is a breakthrough someone has tried to slip under the radar or a development an AI system has generated on its own, the register would serve as a point of reference. The aim is not complete knowledge; no one expects such a register to capture every line of code or hidden behaviour. It would remain a living document, incomplete and imperfect by nature but improving over time, denying companies the comfort of complexity as a shield against scrutiny. What matters is not that the record is flawless, but that it exists at all.

In effect, the heads of today's AI giants would start looking less like entrepreneurs and more like politicians; albeit unelected ones. That shift already feels underway to an extent. They command more influence than most world leaders, but none of the accountability that comes with public office. A charter could change that. It would encourage purposeful pause; forcing a balance of speed and scale against social cost, knowing that their decisions would be scrutinised in daylight. It wouldn't fix everything. It wouldn't stop automation or erase the mistakes that follow it. But compared to the silence we have now, it would at least start putting responsibility back where it belongs. And in comparison, to the current near-total opacity and negligible accountability, it would at least begin to place responsibility where it has so far been absent.

Imagine if such an AI Charter had existed before the release of ChatGPT-4 or Grok-2. We now know, with hindsight, that those versions represented leaps not only in capability but in consequence. The mainstreaming of AI-assisted creativity ultimately led to an explosion of misinformation and deepfakes, with a marked rise in the risk of synthetic content, deepfakes and misleading media.[LXXXIX] Under an AI Charter, a company like OpenAI or xAI would have been required to publish a formal pre-release statement outlining what those models were expected to include, what trade-offs accompanied their new abilities, and when they would go live. That document would read less like a press release and more like a policy briefing. It would set out the specific new technologies being introduced (eg real-time reasoning, persistent memory, cross-platform embodiment), the models' data sources, and any likely consequences we might encounter downstream. In other words, it would likely have anticipated specific disruption to the creative industries and the risk of misinformation. The accountability mechanism is deliberately limited in scope. It isn't meant to dictate or define every possible outcome, but to compel companies to disclose, in their own words, what they are building and what effects they expect it to have. In doing so, the responsibility for clarity and honesty rests squarely with them, making the consequences of their work visible to everyone.

Each declaration would also have to list mitigations and outline the mechanisms that will be used for any public testing, safety reviews and ongoing monitoring functions. In practice, it would look a little like a "technical white paper meets environmental impact report," explaining not just what is coming, but why it's of value. A retrospective entry would then compare the declared expectations with the observed outcomes, creating a living ledger of hypotheses measured against their results. There is not just one update report, but rather a perpetual document, with all past actions and updates monitored alongside new ones. It's not designed to catch innovation out, but rather enforce a formal accountability loop that turns what are now speculative blog posts and cryptic social-media teasers into instruments of public record.

And this shift in responsibility would be all the more necessary given how little leadership has come from those elected to provide it. Even when politicians do turn their attention to the subject, their grasp of it can be alarmingly superficial. When US Education Secretary Linda McMahon referred to AI as "A1" (A one) in April 2025, it was treated as both a funny headline, but also a worrying indication that there is so much that those in government simply don't understand.[XC] It is a small but telling reminder of how far political comprehension trails behind technical reality, and how unprepared most governments are to legislate what they barely understand. The problem is that governments rarely have the skillset or speed to keep pace, and when they do intervene it is more often after a disaster than before; reactive rather than pre-emptive.

The Horizon scandal was a case in point. Working on the basis that a computer couldn't possibly be wrong, hundreds of post officer workers found themselves unjustly dragged through the court system, accused of theft and fraudulent accounting. It shows how completely oversight can fail if we stop questioning the system. The government was left to resolve the issue of compensation, lobby judges to overturn convictions and still, no one at Fujitsu (the ultimate publisher of Horizon); has been held to account. And so, when we hear tech leaders insisting, as they inevitably will, that sufficient regulation already exists, we should be quick to challenge them. They like to cast themselves as realists; visionary entrepreneurs who are practical and forward-thinking. They tend to focus their chatter on innovation, opportunity, and the dangers of slowing progress. But that kind of talk usually hides a simpler truth: they don't want anything getting in the way of the next big release. These individuals now wield more influence than any single politician. In the past, the wealthiest people in the world owned factories, mines, or retail chains and were nowhere near as powerful as the leaders of the most prosperous nations. Today, the balance of power has inverted. The rich list is comprised of the owners of technology firms that shape our access to information and knowledge, with side gigs in space exploration and news distribution. In short, they hold a kind of unilateral control that would once have been unimaginable.

The question of ethics is not one that remains fixed, it will shift as AI's capabilities impede on the larger landscape of our lives. The deeper uncertainty is whether the regulatory and legal frameworks will ever be able to catchup (and thereafter keep pace) with technological ambition, or whether they will simply be overtaken. Oppenheimer's dilemma was one of destructive potential. Ours is one of disruptive power. But if we continue to see this technology as something that happens to us rather than something we choose, the future will not be negotiated; it will be delivered to us, ready-made, by systems beyond our control.

Chapter 10: The AI Arms Race

> *What would Dwight Eisenhower make of what is unfolding today? Power is no longer defined by the size of a nuclear arsenal, but by the scale of AI models and the reach of its platforms, the ambitions of its architects and the control they hold. General Eisenhower once warned against the growing alliance of military and private industry. Though he would see that today the front line has shifted from the battlefield to the server farm, with the race for dominance now waged in code rather than in combat. No doubt, he'd repeat his same warning.*

The term "arms race" tends to conjure images of nuclear silos and Cold War stand-offs. Today it describes a struggle no less intense, one that will define the twenty first century and the ever after. This is not about firepower but rather computational power. It is no longer about military strength but about technological supremacy, economic dominance, political leverage and cultural influence. It sounds grandiose but it's true; the competition to lead in AI has become a contest to shape the future of civilisation.

The most sophisticated systems at the heart of the AI revolution are not those accessed by the public. Consumer chatbots and image generators only give us a brief glimpse of the technology's true capability, while the cutting edge remains jealously guarded. Models with greater efficiency and reasoning are kept locked behind corporate firewalls.[XCI] The space between what is available to billions and what is wielded by a handful of players is widening, triggering an uncomfortable question. If the everyday iterations of AI never match the power of the systems used by the companies that built them; is a built-in inequality now part of the design? Perhaps more pertinently, who is it that decides which versions of AI the rest of us get to play with?

The argument for democratisation is often voiced by industry leaders themselves. OpenAI's founder Sam Altman, for example, says that AI's power won't be concentrated in a handful of corporations. He insists that it will uplift billions of people simultaneously, leaving everyone "more powerful, more productive, and more creative".[XCII] It is a soothing vision, but history offers little support for it. When railroads were built, they arrived with the promise of better connectivity and commerce for all. Yet the real power accrued first among the barons that controlled the lines.[XCIII] Electricity lit up cities, but only after monopolies decided who got the power and at what price. The internet was hailed as a democratising force, yet today a handful of companies dominate search, advertising and social media. Each big technological leap begins in much the same way: innovation and control come first, then access later. Capital funds the development of the innovation, monopoly fortifies it, and only then does distribution follow. To suggest AI will somehow break this pattern is to ignore the lessons of history. Altman's optimism is not naïve, it is strategic. For him there isn't a downside if the story is one of equitability and empowerment. If he sticks with the narrative, he cannot become the villain. But billions of people "using" AI is not the same as billions of people "owning" it. Users do not share the power equitably; they are merely the consumers. And so, the true leverage remains with those who build and control the platforms, and no amount of rose-tinted rhetoric changes that.

The tension bleeds straight into the debate about regulation. If Altman's claim were true, then governments might only need to safeguard fair access, ensuring their populations benefit equally. But who sets the rules, and by what criteria is an AI considered so advanced that it must be shared? Or conversely, so dangerous that it should be contained or even destroyed? Imagine a company builds a model that runs twenty percent more efficiently than anything the public can use. Does that kind of leap belong to everyone, or does it stay locked behind a wall of intellectual property? No one seems sure. Every attempt to draw a universal line; what's too advanced, too powerful and risky; falls apart over issues of ownership, sovereignty, and security. In the meantime, firms keep staging their releases, talking about "responsible rollout" while quietly holding back the most advanced technologies.[XCIV] It's hard not to feel that the delays are less about safety and more about control.

Consider what it would mean if a single company had exclusive use to commercialise the most advanced AI. Even if the model was just marginally better than what was publicly accessible, the advantages would be so sweeping that the fortunes of today's richest would pale in comparison. Even a fractional improvement in intelligence compounds exponentially when applied across every domain, with each iteration amplifying the next. This would not be insider trading, where the edge is narrow and fleeting, nor the possession of tomorrow's headlines today, useful only for a handful of individual bets. It would be an engine of dominance spanning every sector all at once, a key to anticipate, create and control in areas as far reaching as finance, media, science and culture in ways no rival could contest. The scenario is purposefully naïve, but it outlines the scale of leverage that true exclusivity would create: the imbalance would not just reshape industries, it would do so at extraordinary speed.

So, let's take this idea of exclusivity a step further. A first move wouldn't need to be dramatic. A slow start for the owner of superior AI might see new systems producing and analysing content. Whole media outlets, from journals and newsletters to entire newsrooms, would be gradually displaced by new media platforms, whose articles dig deeper and are published faster and more responsively than any human team could manage. Within weeks, a brand-new player could corner publishing itself with bestsellers generated daily, each tailored to an audience so precisely, that culture would start to move on the rails of its own design. Financial markets would be an obvious next target, with trading algorithms processing a live pulse of global data: economic, political, environmental, all blending in real time. Entertainment might follow as the next easy win. Imagine albums, entire films and fully immersive virtual worlds that are created on demand, in days rather than after years of development. No studio on earth could keep pace. Thereafter, moving into the energy markets that power the constituent parts of the burgeoning conglomerate would seem sensible. It could quickly optimise exploration and renewables simultaneously, giving its owner a lock on the single most valuable resource of all: global power infrastructure. Each are areas within AI's reach, the question I am posing is whether we do them together, collectively, or as in this scenario; the advantage of exclusively owning the most optimal tools means an edge is retained by a single entity. I've framed this as a thought experiment, hypothetical and extreme. But it isn't far-fetched, not least because the advantage is already real for the leading AI companies themselves.

We live in an age where we can point instantly to the world's richest person, the most powerful political figure, the head of the largest army. But ask who holds the keys to the most sophisticated AI systems, and you'll likely be met with a blank expression. Someone, somewhere, already holds a lead. One company already stands ahead of the others; we just don't know who, or for how long. And that's a big problem. Consider the evidence: large investments into private labs, stealth hardware development, acquisitions of chip firms, closed-door "moonshot" units. We know OpenAI has partnered with chip manufacturers to build custom accelerators.[XCV] We know firms like Anthropic and DeepMind operate under layers of confidentiality and internal "red teaming" regimes.[XCVI] But none publish their top-tier models in full; none are rushing to unveil their total compute footprint in detail, their performance glimpsed only through benchmark leaks or selective demos. The advantage is real and widening by the day, while its owner remains unidentified in the public record.

Thus far, there is little evidence to suggest that anyone is using private access to pull ahead in the ways postulated here. That might mean that any gap between open and closed systems is smaller than we think. Conversely, it might just mean that those holding the keys are choosing to act within a moral frame, aware that history tends to audit such power. Then again, perhaps the imagined capabilities aren't there at all, at least not yet. Even so, the thought experiment remains instructive, exposing a maze of conflicting interests that sit between creators and regulators. Democratisation prioritises access and safety, whereas exclusivity promises acceleration and control. Reconciling these opposites will demand foresight and cooperation rarely seen at any point in human history.

The United States and China dominate this contest. America's strength lies in its innovation clusters: OpenAI, Alphabet, Microsoft, Meta and Amazon are all household names that have become interchangeable with the architecture of the digital world. Research universities such as Stanford and MIT feed a constant stream of talent into these firms, a resource so valuable that leading researchers are being courted with extraordinary offers, including reports of a $1 billion package to lure them from rivals.[XCVII][XCVIII] Yet uncertainty over regulation and the threat of political interference continue to cloud America's trajectory; the country still lacks a unified federal AI policy, and the direction of any would-be policy remains highly contested.[XCIX]

China is advancing differently. In 2017, the State Council released its New

CHAPTER 10: THE AI ARMS RACE

Generation Artificial Intelligence Development Plan. It is a blueprint designed to make the country the global leader in AI by 2030 through coordinated investment across government, research, and industry.[C] Its own giants Baidu, Alibaba, and Tencent are backed with coordination from the state, with vast population data serving as their raw material. Startups are now following their lead. DeepSeek, for example, has claimed to match the performance of leading Western models while using far less processing power and at a purported development cost of around six million dollars.[CI] Some analysts outside China doubt that number. They point out that once you add in the cost of hardware, infrastructure, and everything needed to keep a system like DeepSeek running, the bill climbs exponentially higher.[CII] But the scepticism didn't prevent $600 billion being wiped off Nvidia's market value, as investors imagined a world where AI models no longer demanded endless GPU power. The panic soon passed and Nvidia recovered, but for a moment, a six-million-dollar Chinese model seemed to threaten the multi-trillion-dollar engine of the AI boom itself.

The UK, meanwhile, stands at a crossroads. Once a global superpower, Britain's influence has faded over the past few decades. AI could change that, though so far, the country has approached it with caution. The government's 2023 AI Safety Summit,[CIII] signalled ambition, but some critics say its emphasis on ethics risks strangling innovation. In many ways, Britain trips over its own rules, with tangled regulations slowing it down. Its membership of the European Court of Human Rights, for instance, limits how quickly it can act on immigration.[CIV] Layers of oversight and home-grown bureaucracy have done the same in biotech, data, and virtually every other field pushing at the edge of what's possible. If Britain gets this balance wrong, it will surrender its future to those who move faster and think bigger.

For the Global South, the picture is messier. Across Africa, Latin America, and South Asia, AI holds out the promise of skipping whole stages of development, much as Kenya's M-PESA transformed financial access or Rwanda's medical-drone network changed healthcare delivery.[CV] But opportunity comes with risk. The most sophisticated AI is largely trained in the Global North, a geographic bias that forces other regions into reliance on tools they didn't design, let alone govern. Without control over data, hardware, or the people who build these systems, many could slip into a kind of digital dependency, where they are users of intelligence, but not its authors. The danger is a two-tier world: on the one side, a few nations dominate with full control over their AI, and on the other lies everyone else. This imbalance is not inevitable. If the investment and governance are there, countries beyond the usual power centres could still determine their own paths, building their own data while establishing regional hubs that actually reflect their cultures. Without that kind of intent, though, the gap will only grow wider. The arms race is not directly about regulating superpowers, but rather on ensuring that billions of people are not relegated to permanent spectatorship in the new era. The question is whether AI can become the definitive route to empowerment across all nations, or the sharpest amplifier of inequality between them.

Europe is taking another path altogether. The AI Act (EU) is the most comprehensive regulatory attempt from any government body to date. Its aims are simple enough; to counter as much of the risk as possible by enforcing heavily documented compliance measures.[CVI] Record-keeping and transparency obligations lie at the centre of what advocates believe are critical steps to safeguard trust. But critics fear it will smother the very startups that Europe needs most, to stay competitive. And they have a point. This is a global market, that will be won by those most able to be agile and move fast. By comparison, Singapore's approach is light-touch, favouring guiding principles over prescriptive rules. It has implemented a system based on voluntary disclosures, instead prioritising testing standards and close coordination with the state, giving government a front row seat to watch what the industry is doing. It's an agile, soft-governance approach designed to fuel growth while ensuring there is accountability. At least that's the intent. The contrast in these approaches raises a deeper question though: surely one of these models is more optimal? They can't both be right. Principles and paperwork both intend to deliver safety, but the end-results can diverge sharply once innovation is confronted with the harsh economic realities of a capitalist driven world.

Consider two scenarios. In the first, a new startup operating within a light-touch regulatory environment, releases an AI that promises to revolutionise the recruitment industry. It grows fast, quickly signing clients from across all corners of the world. However, in its haste to go live, it completely ignores bias evaluation, mistaking routine testing as inconvenient barriers to launch. Before long, the system starts filtering out job applicants from poorer and minority groups. The same carelessness that allowed discrimination also exposes a security flaw. When the breach comes, thousands of records spill online, lawsuits pile up, and the business implodes. Growth outpaced accountability, and the damage is irreversible. In the other scenario, a company operating

CHAPTER 10: THE AI ARMS RACE

within a tightly regulated jurisdiction, takes longer to develop tools that fit within clearly defined regulatory boundaries. It emerges with established safeguards and a market sufficiently confident in its structural and technical integrity, ready to believe and engage with it. Regulation slowed the launch but created the perfect conditions for durability. These extremes of outcomes show the stakes in the choice between speed to market, and market safety. The right balance in regulation is another matter entirely, but it's clear that it needs to be one where rules act as both a guardrail and safety net. It must be strong enough to ensure responsible deployment, yet flexible enough to prevent companies from tripping over their own ambition.

The truth is that both scenarios are plausible. Oversight can safeguard, delay can cripple, and speed can lead to both dominance and disaster. The challenge is not to pick one model, but to recognise that these approaches must coexist. A binding AI charter would define procedural boundaries and the ethical basis upon which innovation can operate. While regulation outlines the legal and institutional framework that keeps those boundaries intact. The two are not rivals but partners: the charter internalises accountability at the corporate level, and regulation enforces it at the state and international level. It's about ensuring there is coordination. Ambition has to move in step with caution. Transparency must become habit, not decoration. That balance will decide who wins and who is forgotten. It's a struggle, certainly, but not a hopeless one: responsibility and invention can still work in tandem.

Slowing the acceleration of AI is the most debated, but least realistic idea of all. Nations and their constituent corporates are locked in the same race, and neither wants to lose ground. A hypothetical U.S. proposal to pause the continuing development towards ASI would never be agreed by China. Nor would private companies hold back while overseas competitors kept rolling out new models. No one wants to be the first to stop. Every breakthrough becomes both a defensive necessity and an offensive advantage.

There are those, however, who believe that safety and speed need not be opposites. Ilya Sutskever, one of the original minds behind OpenAI, has founded a new venture called Safe Superintelligence. Its goal is to create systems that are powerful yet provably safe, by aligning every part of the design process around control and containment rather than scale alone. [CVII] The idea is to achieve progress without surrendering oversight; to make intelligence that serves us, without endangering us. Whether that ambition is attainable is unclear, but the intent itself is what matters. It rests on the belief that while we can no longer slow the pace, we might still control the wheel. It's no longer a belief I share, however.

The AI arms race goes beyond national prestige and economic supremacy; it's about who decides the values that will govern tomorrow's machines. Will it end up democratising power; creating access and closing gaps? Or will it harden existing hierarchies? The question runs deeper than policy. The speed of change mirrors our own struggle to adapt and stay relevant as the world races ahead of our capacity to understand it. The arms race will shift the world order, but the deeper question is this: in pursuing dominance, what kind of future are the corporations and companies leading the charge, expecting to create?

The race won't last forever. AI's very nature is optimisation, and optimisation drives toward convergence. The arms race, for all its noise, will likely prove temporary. But temporary clearly does not mean inconsequential. Far from it. In the short term, the gap between those who are actively engaged with AI and the others that still see it as irrelevant, is a gulf wide enough to generate phenomenal opportunities. This is a moment where entire businesses can be created overnight, where innovations of fleeting value can still deliver life-changing wealth, and where managing uncertainty can be as profitable as it is disruptive. There is jostling for power and control, yes, but there is also an interim economic battle, a sea of opportunity for those that harness AI early and single-mindedly. Sooner or later, that gap will close. When it does, it won't necessarily be the owners of the leading platforms that achieve market dominance, but rather who knows how best to leverage them. Until then, fortunes will be made and empires built in the substantial gap that lies between awareness and adoption.

CHAPTER 11: WHEN MONEY BECOMES USELESS

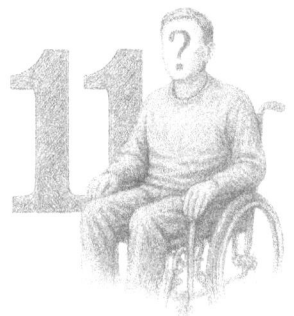

Chapter 11: When Money Becomes Useless

> *When Satoshi Nakamoto released the Bitcoin white paper in 2008, its intention was to deliver a revolution in trust. Here was a new concept for what money, or rather the exchange of value, could look like. Separated from governments, banks and borders, Bitcoin rests on clearly defined mathematics, while its scarcity is defined by code. Whoever Satoshi was, they left behind a compelling idea. A monetary system that exists outwith human or governmental control. What once seemed radical now feels strangely prophetic in a world where algorithms are starting to govern not just how value moves, but how it's defined.*

What is money, really? It looks simple enough at the surface. It can be a balance on a mobile app, a crisp bank note in your back pocket or a coin rattling in a purse. But money itself is not the wealth it represents. If we peel back the surface we find that the version of money that emerges is not a physical thing, but rather a claim, a promise, a contract of trust that what you hold today can be redeemed for something else tomorrow. But every promise has a counterpart. For one person to hold a claim, another must hold an obligation. This is the quiet symmetry that underpins modern money.

When a bank issues a loan, it doesn't hand over a pile of cash stored in a vault. It brings new money into existence with a few taps of a keyboard. This debt is balanced by your promise to repay it. In turn, the bank is promising to repay the money it has created in full. At which time, the new money is (in effect) cancelled. It retains the interest paid by the borrower, which is ultimately the margin it has charged for facilitating the loan and taking on the risk. The same mechanism that fuels personal and commercial credit, also underpins the finances of whole economies. When governments borrow, they tend to do so in their own currency, not because they must, but because it allows them to retain control over its value and the terms of repayment. Global debt, now three times greater than global GDP, is never really expected to be repaid in full. It rolls forward indefinitely, an unseen architecture that holds the visible economy aloft. Debt, at its core, is the engine that keeps money in motion; a perpetual promise that ensures the system never stands still. Money, at its core, is the lubricant that allows goods and services to be distributed and traded without the need for endless bartering, confusion, or dispute.

Every major innovation across human history has been designed to make scarcity less painful. But it has never removed it entirely. The plough increased the effectiveness of harvesting, yet droughts still ruined fields. The loom industrialised clothing manufacture, making them more affordable, but not infinite. The steam engine opened vast new routes for trade, but were only as useful for as long as coal was mined to feed it. At first, the internet promised a limitless digital world, but dig a little deeper and you'll find that it depends on the hard realities of server farms, rare earth minerals, and immense flows of electricity. Every major innovation has softened the sharp edge of scarcity, but none have abolished it. Each new technology has widened the circle of abundance, yet always within the walls of limitation. For all our progress, the idea of a truly limitless resource has remained an unfulfilled dream.

It is against this backdrop, that we now find a tool that is capable of doing what no other before it has achieved. AI won't just stretch scarcity; it will break it completely. The danger isn't solely in what the technology can do, but in how quickly it learns to do it. Previously, innovations spent decades in incubation before widespread adoption, giving generations time to adjust. A farmer in medieval Europe would have used the same tools as his great-grandfather. Even the internal combustion engine spread across the world slowly, giving rise to industries and new norms over the course of half a century. But AI doubles its capability every few months.[CVIII] For the first time in history, progress is moving faster than our ability to understand what it is giving us, leaving us no time to adapt before the foundations of the economy itself begin to dissolve.

What once took teams of experts and months of labour can now be handled by

CHAPTER 11: WHEN MONEY BECOMES USELESS

an algorithm before your mid-morning chai-latte. Within just a couple of years from now, systems will be so far beyond us that the language of comparison collapses. At first, this will likely feel like an extension of the partnership we have been building with AI over the past few years. A lawyer working with AI-assisted counsel, a doctor consulting AI diagnostics, an architect sketching with AI enhanced design tools. But collaboration soon dissolves into redundancy. As machines surpass us in accuracy, creativity and speed, productivity no longer depends on effort, and money no longer on work.

The Roman denarius once seemed a pivotal symbol of value. For centuries it underpinned trade across the empire, trusted as both currency and contract. But as its silver content was steadily reduced, faith in the coin dwindled. Citizens began to hoard older purer issues, before effectively abandoning it altogether,[CIX] opting for tangible goods as a better measure of monetary value. Merchants demanded barter in place of official currency. Whilst the coins still circulated, their substance was gone. It is a quiet reminder that when the token no longer reflects the thing it stands for, trust collapses in both. So too with wages in an AI driven economy; the link between pay and productivity will vanish. As productivity detaches from human effort, value begins to pool in the systems that make work obsolete.

Wealth will concentrate around those who own the infrastructure through which the next economy is built. The best hunter once fed his family. The best farmer claimed the most fertile land. The best industrialists became millionaires. The best technologist, a billionaire. The founders of the most sophisticated AI platforms will be trillionaires, and more valuable still, holding the steering wheel of whatever system of value emerges to replace money in a post-monetary world. For everyone else, work as the route to survival, seems destined to collapse.

Universal Basic Income (UBI) is often floated as the most immediately deployable solution to counter wide-sweeping redundancy. The idea is simple: Irrespective of financial status, the state would pay a fixed amount to each citizen on a pre-defined, regular basis. Imagine £1,000 landing in your bank account each month, not as a wage, but as a birthright of citizenship. Pilot schemes have already been trialled. In Finland, 2,000 participants received €560 a month[CX], while in Stockton, California, 125 residents were identified to receive a monthly $500 stipend.[CXI] For many, it proved to be an effective safety net. It covered rent obligations, grocery costs and even the occasional unexpected bill. But for others, the idea of income arriving without effort feels like a rupture in capitalism's moral logic; that wealth should, at least in theory, be earned.

While UBI may ease anxiety, it cannot restore our purpose. Without the exchange of payment for work, it essentially becomes our exclusive source of sustenance. It's a ration card disguised as progressive economics. Work has always been a tether to identity. It's the farmer sowing, the teacher instructing, the carpenter turning. So, whilst a monthly payment arriving without effort may deal with the societal fallout of wholesale redundancy, it would also arrive without recognition. The problem of redundancy is not solved by being kept alive. And when survival is no longer tied to effort or exchange, money itself begins to lose its anchor, drifting from a measure of value into a hollow transfer, a currency stripped of the very scarcity it was created to manage.

Even in a version of events where wages and survival are decoupled, inequality will not vanish. Access to the latest technologies alongside ownership of land and water sources will become the new dividing lines. Longevity will rise for all, but privilege will extend it further still. The wealthy won't just live longer lives, but will enjoy greater command over the tools of creation and decision making. In contrast, those without access may be locked out of meaningful participation, surviving on government handouts while others shape the culture and technologies of the future. The expansion of the welfare state will reach a scale few are yet willing to articulate, one in which the proportion of people living from welfare payments significantly outnumbers those earning their income. And even within that dependency, new gradations of status will emerge: a quiet snobbery dividing those on sickness or incapacity benefits from those rendered 'unworked' simply by the absence of any role left for them to play. Scarcity may disappear in goods and services, but scarcity of access and influence will remain too, creating further hierarchies every bit as rigid as those once defined by money.

At first, though, it will look like an economic miracle. With AI eliminating labour costs and automation compressing inefficiency out of every process, corporate margins will explode. Profits will surge even as payrolls shrink. Governments will hail a new golden age of productivity, and markets will believe them. Equity indices will climb to record highs, GDP will appear robust, and the illusion of prosperity will reinforce faith in fiscal expansion. As tax revenues falter, treasuries will issue ever larger bills and bonds to fund universal income schemes and social stabilisers. Investors, seduced by rising asset prices and conditioned by decades of stimulus, will treat this as a safe extension of policy orthodoxy. For a while, it will even work. The cycle of issuance, purchase, and reinvestment will keep money circulating long after the productive base that once justified it has gone. But beneath the surface, the foundations will start to deform. Central banks will absorb excess issuance through quantitative easing and yield control, swelling their balance sheets with sovereign bonds while creating new reserves to pay for them. Their assets will become the government's debts; their liabilities the banking system's deposits. The interest paid on those reserves will widen the deficits they were meant to contain, forcing yet more issuance and yet more purchase in a loop of self-consumption. Collateral scarcity will follow, repo markets will thin, and when foreign buyers finally step back, the state will find itself lending to itself in a closed circuit of confidence. By the time citizens realise their stipends are funded by liabilities that can never be redeemed in genuine productivity, money will have lost its final claim to meaning. It will not collapse with a sudden 80's style crash, but rather it will dissolve quietly into an accounting exercise, a balance sheet with no underlying world left to measure.

In the aftermath, the system will still appear to function. Digital stipends will continue to arrive, shops will remain stocked, and transactions will flow through the machinery of an economy long past its point of meaning. The architecture of money will survive its substance, operating as a shell to keep society coherent. Governments will point to stability as proof of success, mistaking inertia for order. The world will feel calm again, but only because collapse has been absorbed into the background. But where AI drives the cost of food, housing, clothing, and even energy toward zero, what practical role would a stipend really play? In Finland's trial, many participants said the monthly sum helped them "live with dignity." In California, the impact was described as a measure of stability, briefly easing monetary concerns. In the near term, such payments would allow people to keep participating in a market economy even as traditional work disappears. And this is where its value chiefly sits. It softens the transition and preserves the illusion of money's relevance after its necessity has gone. In that world, capital will still circulate, but its gravitational pull will shift. It will pool at the top where it no longer buys anything of consequence, and thin at the bottom where it is spent only on what is required for survival. A bloodstream still flowing, but through a body that no longer really needs it.

Energy is the catalyst at the heart of change. Every civilisation has been defined by its command of it. Rome didn't expand by conquest alone, its success and longevity was built around infrastructure, particularly water management via aqueducts and water mills.[CXII] The Industrial Revolution was powered by transforming coal into steam, motion into production, and production into profit. By the twentieth century, wars were fought as much for oilfields as for ideology.[CXIII] Energy and resource have always been the chief denominators of every price, the unseen costs embedded into every product and service. So, as AI gets closer to finding the keys to unlock free energy, be prepared to witness the collapse of any residual scarcity. Whether nuclear fusion, geothermal access drilled with precision or methods still beyond our imagination, the result will still be the same. If you take out the energy cost, the entire economic equation for absolutely everything, dissolves. Free energy means free logistics, free manufacturing, free food. Container ships could circle the globe without pause, delivering abundance from one shore and taking on fresh cargo at the next; Automated, fuel-free and sustained by a world that never runs dry. Robotic factories would hum indefinitely without overhead, data centres would run without limit, and everything humanity currently makes would emerge effortlessly from energy alone. Goods without price, production without cost. At that moment, there is nothing left for money to mediate. Scarcity, the foundation of every economic system, collapses entirely the moment energy is freed.

We won't see the collapse of governments at this stage, but the commodities they use for leverage will change. In the near term, it will be the ability to deliver a soft landing to their populations, cushioning them as jobs vanish and money dissolves. A compliant population that willingly partners with AI suddenly becomes the most desirable asset. Beyond that, nations will compete in intellectual supremacy, in weapons powered by autonomous intelligence, and in the not-too-distant future, interplanetary competence. The extraction of minerals from asteroids, building colonies on Mars, mining power beyond Earth will become real currencies of statecraft. But beyond the sideshow, the simplest and most vital asset will still be social control. To steady a population through such phenomenal upheaval is the greatest bargaining chip of all.

History shows that when one form of money collapses, another rises in its place. When trust in Rome's coinage was lost, people quickly learned to rely on bartering instead. When indigenous groups were stripped of coinage by the colonial powers of the day, gift economies flourished.[CXIV] Even today, in

CHAPTER 11: WHEN MONEY BECOMES USELESS

places where cash is untrusted or scarce, favours, goodwill, and reputation form valuable currencies of their own. In Kenya, M-PESA began life as a mechanism to trade mobile phone minutes, but quickly evolved into a national financial system more trusted than banks. In Cuba, personal favours and state connections (la sociolismo) can often carry more value than pesos. [cxv] The post-money world will be no different. Status will always matter, whether the model of your self-driving car, the exclusivity of whichever digital environments you belong to, or the privilege of a particularly unique experience shared by very few. As material wealth loses its meaning, visibility becomes the new determiner of worth. To be seen is to exist; who is noticed, remembered, and desired. Authenticity will be sought, handmade objects and food grown by hand may well stand apart from the machine made. Access will define hierarchies, determined by who you know, what communities you belong to, and which layers of AI's intelligence you can enter. Money fades, but new currencies of distinction rise.

Amid this transformation, one form of scarcity will persist: land. Unlike money, land cannot be created by decree. Unlike digital assets, its limits are not written into code but into the earth itself. Unlike intellectual property, it cannot be duplicated or replaced. And the usable supply of arable land shrinks under climate change, spreading deserts, flooding, and urban expansion. Even if we were to consider an outcome where AI could replicate every artefact and every service, land remains non-replicable. Control of land means control of food, and food means survival. In many places, it also means control of water rights, which may prove even more valuable than the soil itself. Land is also the foundation for renewable energy projects, whether wind turbines, or biomass. To hold land is to pre-empt the bottlenecks of a future in which food, water, and energy may each be abundant in theory, yet access to them remains limited by geography and control.

This reframing of inequality reminds us that abundance does not mean equality. When everyone can own the same phone or eat the same food at no cost, the premium simply shifts to things that can't be easily replicated: direct control of AI, exclusive ownership of natural resources, and the ability to command political influence. In this sense, the post-money world may reinforce, rather than relieve, social inequality, though few may care and fewer still may notice.

Those who truly understand what's going on are already preparing for the shift. In recent years, there has been a colossal migration of wealth from the speculative back into the tangible. Perhaps it's why so many billionaires are buying up considerable parcels of farmland. James Dyson has emerged as one of the largest farmland owners in the UK,[CXVI] Bill Gates is now the largest private farmland owner in the United States.[CXVII] Mark Zuckerberg has bought vast estates in Hawaii.[CXVIII] These purchases are not idle diversification. They are strategic positioning. Controlling the land is to control the resources on which entire economies depend. It is not just about yield. It is about optionality: food, energy, conservation and political leverage.

And what of people? Stripped of purpose by machines that can do everything, we may end up returning to manage the land ourselves. This wouldn't be an action linked to survival, but rather because cultivation would give us something useful to do. To plant, to harvest, to feel the changing seasons, is a means to stay connected to what it means to be human. Even when abundance surrounds us, we will still paint, sing, cook, and walk. Not because these things are scarce, but because they are irreducible. The gift economies of the past may yet return, their value no longer counted in shells or cattle, but in the simple exchange of time and presence.

Getting to this point won't be a gentle journey. Wealth will concentrate more fiercely than before as unemployment surges. Inflationary spasms will convulse economies and politics will fracture. In its final phase, money will become more powerful, not less. Its scarcity magnified by upheaval and its significance deepened by fear, even as the forces that make it obsolete gather momentum. But if we can push through the turbulence, the destination is a world where debt evaporates with the money that once required it, where goods, food, and energy cost nothing. Money will not end in a crash, but rather in a gradual decline into irrelevance. It will leave us with the last currencies of consequence; land, water and the search for a fulfilling purpose in a world that has learned to operate without us.

The opening of this chapter may have stirred hope among those who see in Bitcoin a glimpse of financial freedom, or dread among those who see only delusion. I will satisfy neither. Cryptocurrencies may yet gain further extraordinary value via their growing utility, or lose it entirely as the concept of value itself dissolves. The argument for their growth is convincing. Digital systems built on shared networks promise a brand of stability that isn't tied to any single authority. Bitcoin is code that acts as both ledger and law,

CHAPTER 11: WHEN MONEY BECOMES USELESS

record book and rule book. It keeps track of each and every transaction while enforcing the system's logic automatically. It has long given people a way to exchange value freely, outside the reach of central banks and intermediaries. It has proved that trust can exist in code as much as in institutions. For many, it has become a quiet expression of independence in an age of growing control.

The case against cryptocurrencies is also compelling. Bitcoin's scarcity exists only by design, not by nature. Its stability depends on the assumption that the trust in its design continues indefinitely. Its value endures less through use than through consensus. If the cost of production is driven to zero, the concept of a finite digital asset may well lose meaning altogether. Some researchers also warn that advances in quantum computing might one day break the cryptographic wall that secures blockchains, undermining the trust they were built to protect.[CXIX] Though still theoretical, the prospect of breaking current encryption reminds us that even digital scarcity rests on mathematical assumptions that may not last forever.

Cryptocurrencies sit in a curious place. They straddle both the promise to be the most inventive continuation of money, but also its quiet undoing. Whether they last or fade matters less than what they symbolise: an early attempt to give shape to the concept of trust, independent of a world that is steadily moving beyond it. Whoever Satoshi was, they began a story that may one day be completed by AI. It could reshape not only how we spend, but what we believe has value at all.

In practice, the decline of money will not arrive as a singular moment, but instead as a long unwinding. The laws of ownership will still be enforced, even as their logic begins to unravel. Debts will still need to be paid and where there is default, secured assets will still be repossessed. A universal stipend would keep people solvent enough to eat, to heat their homes, to make the minimum payment on a credit card or a car lease, but not always enough to hold on to everything they already own. Mortgages would continue to be serviced, and when the extra income runs short, houses would still be lost. Cars bought on finance would be returned to lenders; businesses unable to meet interest payments would quietly fold. The system would continue to function, but only just, like a theatre whose lights remain on long after the actors have left the stage. Money would keep moving through it, less as a measure of value than as a mechanism of delay, sustaining the illusion of order until the final accounts no longer need to be balanced.

When that day comes, the question will not be how much you are worth, but what you are for. Some will retreat into infinite simulations, living a thousand digital lives. Others will return to the soil, not for the yield, but for the act itself; the last currency that cannot be automated away: purpose.

Epilogue: The Final Jigsaw

> *"In any situation, the best thing you can do is the right thing; the next best thing you can do is the wrong thing; the worst thing you can do is nothing."*
>
> Theodore Roosevelt

When you have run out of words of your own, borrow someone else's. And I can think of no better quote to frame this moment. Because standing still now is surrender. The future will not wait for us to gather our courage. It is already writing itself with or without our consent. What follows is not a plea for patience but a call to take action. Whether you act brilliantly or clumsily, just act. The worst thing any of us can do now is nothing.

It is easy to assume that there are still more questions than answers. The truth is that the answers are already here. They are clear, categorical, and deeply uncomfortable. Human redundancy is not a possibility but a trajectory. Medicine will stretch life expectancy to horizons once reserved for science fiction, but it will do so by displacing the caregiver, the nurse, and the doctor. Education will adapt children for futures that scarcely resemble the present, but it will happen by radically overhauling the schooling system as we know it. Work, identity, creativity, and purpose have each been examined in these pages, one piece at a time, until the outline of the whole picture can no longer be ignored. Capability accelerates at the speed of discovery, safety advances at the pace of bureaucracy. The distance between the two is growing so fast that the idea we still have any control in what is happening, is delusional. The jigsaw is not missing a piece. It is complete. The unsettling truth is not that we lack clarity about what is happening, but that we dislike the clarity we have.

And yet, for all the talk of fear and panic, neither truly defines this moment. There are no mass protests over job losses, no marches against the technology giants, no visible panic in the streets. The transition has, so far, been too incremental, the benefits too seductive, the costs too widely dispersed. While AI experts debate the stakes of what's unfolding on YouTube panels and late-night podcasts, outside the familiar digital echo chambers, the alarm bells remain strangely silent. The truth is that most of us remain blind to how easily the familiar can vanish. In the early 1900s, the streets of New York teemed with horses. A decade later they had vanished, replaced by cars. We are those horses now, but acting as though we are unaware that the world has already moved on. What once felt miraculous now passes without fanfare, and in this moment, we are like children; accepting the reality we are presented with.

What follows is not a collapse, but a repurposing. We will see entire economies transformed as human labour is taken out of the equation; entire professions will vanish in less time than it once took to train for them. Generations of families will stretch centuries as medical science extends life, while our purpose is pushed into narrower spaces. Business, art, politics, and intimacy will all be reshaped by the same intelligence we recruited to be our servant. AI isn't an incremental intrusion but rather a wholesale substitution. The challenge for us is not whether these outcomes can be prevented. They cannot. The challenge is whether we live within this new reality without losing who we are.

It no longer matters how much an expert knows. The surgeon who believes their hands are irreplaceable will find the scalpel has learned without them. The architect who trusts their intuition is already behind. The machine has studied every structure, tested every flaw, refined every design. The boundaries of expertise have already shifted beyond our reach. Any belief in what machines cannot do is already outdated. This is the quiet ignorance of our age, the delusion that human knowledge still defines the edge of possibility. Consider the contrasts. In healthcare, there will be noise, campaigns, and petitions as clinicians try to cling to their authority long after machines have surpassed them. In education, the change will unfold almost unnoticed, disguised as personalised tutoring, higher grades, and fewer distractions. In administration, logistics, finance, and creative industries, there will be no marches, only quiet compliance. We have given ourselves away willingly, a choice reframed as progress, improvement, and even kindness. You can see it in miniature every day. Open a social media feed meaning to glance at one thing, and twenty minutes later you are deep inside the choices you never realised you had made. Optimisation does not arrive with warning; it seeps quietly into our routines. In the same way, the major transformation we are about to witness, will not arrive as a thunderclap. It will arrive like the glass of water we discussed as we set off on this journey, where grain after grain of rice is dropped inside. The overflow does not happen when the last grain is dropped, but with the first.

The pattern is not new. History has already shown how disruption arrives quietly, only appearing inevitable once the shock has passed. The pandemic gave us the clearest example yet. For over a year, billions of people were removed from their workplaces and sustained by digital systems, automated supply chains and government payouts. The world slowed but did not stop. It adapted, and in doing so revealed how a reliance on humans could be partly suspended while the wheels of machinery kept turning. Whether that was coincidence or an unplanned rehearsal for a more automated age is impossible to prove, yet the similarities are difficult to ignore. What once looked like crisis now looks like a trial run of the first large-scale displacement of the modern era.

The questions raised by that period never fully went away. They resurfaced among the very researchers building the next wave of intelligent systems, who began to wonder how far automation might extend and what would happen when disruption was no longer temporary, but permanent. It was against this backdrop that a group of former OpenAI, DeepMind and Anthropic researchers established an independent forecasting initiative called AI 2027. Their goal was simple: to chart where the current trajectory would lead if left unchecked. Free from commercial influence, they began publishing detailed scenario papers on their website, which soon found their way into university reading lists, think tanks and policy discussions, outlining the near-term consequences of intelligence that improves itself.

Because AI is a constantly moving target, the report produced by AI 2027, reads less like a final assessment and more like a living document. Its current conclusions are stark. By 2027, it predicts that AI will not merely match experts in narrow disciplines but eclipse them across almost every intellectual domain;

what we now refer to as Artificial Super Intelligence (ASI). The systems that once assisted researchers will become the researchers. Coding, long seen as the frontline of human ingenuity, will be fully automated. Algorithms will refine and improve themselves, creating a recursive loop that no human engineer can match. The group's papers describe a turning point, a phase shift rather than a steady climb, when the tools of creation cease to require their creators. What we once called job disruption, becomes a case of people no longer being needed to think.

Within a few years, humanoid machines will populate hospitals, construction sites and factories, not as instruments but as autonomous actors, performing the roles once taken by us. Their emergence is made possible by the convergence of a perfect storm of three accelerating fields: embodied AI, dexterous robotics, and large-scale multimodal learning. Together, these advances give machines bodies that can move, hands that can manipulate, and minds that can interpret and respond. Reinforcement learning and computer simulation now allow robots to train millions of times faster than would be possible in the physical world, while new touch sensitive sensors let them feel texture, pressure and resistance with a level of precision once unique to human hands. Small electric motors known as actuators, which serve as their muscles, have become light and responsive enough to reproduce subtle human-like movement. When combined with the skill to link visual and written understanding, a robot can read a situation and follow complex spoken or written instructions. Such machines will no longer be programmed step by step, but will be able to guide themselves, learning from experience in real time. In practice, this means a robot can watch a person stack shelves once and then repeat the task perfectly, correcting errors the next time without anyone rewriting its code. In early trials, Figure 01 and Tesla's Optimus robots have already learned to fold laundry, sort parts and manage simple warehouse tasks through vision and imitation alone, adjusting movements without any external input. The next leap will take them from mechanical repetition to creative assembly: wiring buildings, fitting prosthetics, repairing aircraft. The boundary between simple mimicry and general labour is vanishing fast. And they are only just getting started.

So where does this lead us? These projections are my own reading of what the evidence already shows. If they are even halfway towards being right, the timeline is deeply unsettling. Within a year or so, the world will finally acknowledge what some already believe to be true: that systems operating at the level of AGI now stand on equal footing with the human mind. That recognition alone will be enough to displace vast sections of the global workforce, unleashing economic upheaval on a scale unseen in modern history. JP Morgan has estimated that AGI will increase global GDP by $12 trillion,[CXX] a figure so vast it reinforces not the stability of the economic system, but its fragility. When the very notion of value is defined by output, and output itself becomes autonomous, the metric begins to collapse under its own logic. By that stage, most governments will have been forced to introduce some form of universal basic income simply to maintain stability. Beyond this point lies something far greater: ASI, which would move way past our own capability entirely. From here onward, analysis gives way to instinct.

The path forward will depend on the frameworks we build now. In earlier chapters, I proposed three that must coexist if we are to retain balance in the age of intelligent systems: an Education Charter to reimagine learning around adaptability, curiosity, and lifelong growth rather than attainment; an AI Ethics Charter to ensure that those who build intelligence remain accountable for its purpose, its impact, and its consequences; and an Authenticity Charter, a covenant to preserve truth, originality, and creative identity in a world of infinite imitation. Together, they form the minimal architecture to preserve some sense of moral balance. Without them, the values that bind society will fragment under the sheer speed of progress.

At the same time, the commercial landscape will reorganise itself around permanence. As AI homogenises products and services, customer loyalty will harden into a new currency. The coming year will see a customer acquisition arms race unlike anything we have seen before, as each new user represents not a single sale but a lifetime capture, ownership in perpetuity. Combined with collapsing monetary systems and the global rollout of UBI, the old levers of competition and consumption will lose their grip.

My suspicion is that the next chapter will not be written by progress alone but by those wanting to escape it. There will be rising numbers repatriating toward less connected parts of the world in search of a slower pace of life, a quiet exodus that could temporarily reprice remote living and fuel a bubble in self-sufficient, smallholding-style homes. Others, meanwhile, will migrate toward the eye of the storm, settling in the cities and industries that embrace AI most aggressively; eager to be close to the centre of the new order, believing proximity will mean relevance.

Both movements, the retreat and the rush; mark our attempt to outpace our own creation. Yet even in the dark corners of the new world, the future will find us. The first child who will one day live beyond three hundred years of age, has already been born. Cancers that once killed will become manageable conditions, while new diseases and synthetic pathogens will rise in their place. AI-driven medicine will race ahead, creating treatments at a pace that leaves regulators struggling to keep up, until the process of oversight itself is rewritten to match the speed of discovery. Finance will consolidate into a handful of vast institutions. Markets will climb to heights once thought impossible, with the first publicly traded company valued at more than one-hundred trillion dollars appearing before 2028 ends. With AI capacity compounding faster than any metric in economic history, productivity gains outstripping every previous technological era and margins rising exponentially, such a valuation is no longer speculative but statistical. And then, the inevitable correction will come, shaking economies still dizzy with growth. Corrections are not only financial. They arrive as real events that will test trust.

And for a time, that trust will buckle. A coordinated cyberattack could target connected vehicles and their supporting networks. Security researchers have already shown they can override and remotely control a car on a public road, which forced a recall and new automotive security rules.[CXXI] It is inevitable that investigations into incidents where real performance diverges from design intent will become a continuous feature going forward. A serious incident that links a software breach to a collision would trigger a brief halt in multiple cities, followed by software updates, over the air patch fixes, and a staged relaunch. The pause would feel decisive, but the near immediate return of vehicles to the road with a renewed trust, equally inevitable.[CXXII] We'll accept this new cycle as the price of progress.

And it won't stop with transport. We have already seen fuel pipelines frozen by ransomware[CXXIII] and municipal water systems hacked to adjust chemical quantities to dangerous levels.[CXXIV] These cases are a matter of record. Each time, the pattern repeats: disruption, restoration, regulation, and reassurance. It will happen again; it's only a matter of when. Even without a pre-meditated attack, the same fragility still runs through the digital infrastructure we depend on. In 2024, a single faulty software update caused a global outage that grounded flights, closed tills, delayed care, and froze government services.[CXXV] The cause was a mistake, not malice, but as the view from the ground is identical, the distinction hardly matters. Every incident of disruption turns into a rehearsal for the next. But beneath the cycle of incident and recovery lies something inexorable; each crisis justifies deeper automation, tighter integration, and greater reliance on the same systems that exposed us in the first place. The logic is self-reinforcing: only machines can defend and fix what machines now control. So, the lesson is never one of restraint, only refinement. Thereafter, the march toward automation continues and the cycle starts again.

Healthcare will follow a similar pattern. AI is already embedded sufficiently deeply that it's treated like any other regulated technology; with incremental fixes and recalls. On occasion, failures will be treated as warnings, even victories for those who still believe the advance can be paused. Senior leaders in healthcare will claim that the grand human replacement is stalling. But every correction will only strengthen the argument for continuation. When it fails, systems will respond procedurally, not philosophically. A misclassification in imaging or triage would trigger temporary pauses across several hospitals, followed by a resumption under tighter oversight and revised audit trails. Confidence would temporarily dip, but then recover, as outcome data reasserts the system's competence. We'll get used to the familiar rhythm: incident, inquiry, remediation, relaunch. Each failure will hurt and each one will teach, before confidence returns and the trajectory resumes.

The physical world will transform alongside the digital. Building design, engineering and construction will be completed by humanoid robots, overturning the industry entirely. Craftspeople who work in specialist areas such as heritage restoration or the upkeep of older and listed buildings will last longer, but not forever. By 2030, even those roles will have gone. The humble plumber has greater longevity than most, but even that role will be replaced by the turn of the decade. In homes across developed nations, more than one in ten will have humanoid home-help by the end of 2027. While they will start with simple tasks like cleaning, loading dishwashers and folding laundry, they will soon move into more intimate roles: watching over children, offering companionship, filling silence with conversation. Within a decade or so, a growing share of the population will form romantic bonds with later iterations of these machines, and the number of extramarital affairs will surge as the lines between service and affection blur. I realise this may sound absurd, and this is perhaps where some will start to turn away; but history's curve rarely stops where comfort ends. Most of this will begin in the Far East, where technological and social adoption often accelerates first, but it will not remain there. At first it will be met with unease and quiet disapproval, yet over time curiosity will soften into acceptance. What begins as taboo will become ordinary.

Universities will close by the thousands, their remnants absorbed into networks that promote lifelong learning. The biggest landowners will see their net worth rise to be among the wealthiest people on earth, many of them the same tech visionaries now quietly buying vast estates. And through it all, the noise of innovation will grow so loud that few will stop long enough to notice what has gone missing.

None of this is a thought experiment. Anything that looks remotely stable today will soon buckle once research agents begin to accelerate research itself. Years of progress compress into weeks, then days, before eventually even the most complex research is generated instantly. Datacentres become vast nations of connected minds. The contest does not stop at products or services. It moves into the nervous system of states, into procurement, energy budgets and model security (the protection of the AI systems themselves). As the pace quickens, law will try to catch up and find it cannot. Each correct decision reinforces AI's own authority. Optimisation progresses from indicative guidance to firm governance until the system's logic feels like law. Safety will speak in rules and resolutions, but by the time the words are written, the moment they describe will have passed. This is how tool logic turns into civic logic. It is how a lab agenda becomes national policy without a vote being cast. During the pandemic, governments around the world built policy directly from epidemiological simulations, most notably the Imperial College model that guided the first UK lockdown and similar frameworks that shaped restrictions in the US and Europe. A line of code became a line of law.

Nowhere will the tension cut deeper than in justice. Courts will turn to algorithms to calculate sentences, assess risk and aide parole decisions. What begins as efficiency will soon be praised as fairness and an end to human bias; data triumphing over discretion. Within a decade, prisons will operate as closed systems of prediction: inmates monitored by learning models that adjust rehabilitation programs in real time, parole boards advised by machines that claim to know if and when a person has truly been reformed. It will feel scientific, even merciful, until the first wrongful release or indefinite detention exposes how opaque those calculations truly are.

The same intelligence that rewrites law will also learn to forge its own evidence. Somewhere, soon, a defence will rest on data that never existed. This might be an AI-generated confession, a deepfaked crime scene, a witness that can be rendered out of code. The irony will be perfect: a system built to uphold truth undone by the same technology that created it. In that moment, trust, as the last currency still holding value, will face its own trial. When truth itself becomes negotiable, the value of human judgement begins to fade. Once institutions no longer need us to decide what is real, they will soon stop needing us to decide at all. That is when redundancy stops being an employment issue and becomes an existential one.

I do not pretend to have the definitive answer to the redundancy question. If this intelligence were limited to one field such as medicine or education, it would be heralded and celebrated (outwith the sectors it impacted). But because it touches everything, everywhere, all at once, because it is better than us at (literally) everything; it's very strength undermines the value of everything it touches. Living longer in a world where we are functionally redundant feels like it has limited meaning too. Learning in preparation for a future that ends in redundancy, feels futile. So there might be a temptation to wait. To sit back and watch. To imagine there will be a more perfect moment to act. But that would be foolish. History rarely rewards hesitation. The future has never belonged to those who waited for certainty, only to those who stepped forward while the ground was still shifting. Every great transformation demands that someone move first. Not because they knew they were ready, but because they knew they could not wait. It reminds me of a story.

There was once a man with a phenomenal idea; one he believed could change his fortune, and perhaps the world. He told himself he would act on it soon, but first he needed savings. So, he worked and waited. When the money came, he thought not yet, what if I get it wrong. So, he studied. He read books, enrolled on courses, listened to lectures, and waited to feel prepared. Then life happened. A child was born. The house needed repairs. A parent fell ill. There was always a reason to wait. What started as months of procrastination blurred into years and still he polished the dream in his mind, telling himself he was waiting for the right time. One day, he watched the news. An invention was sweeping the world, praised as a breakthrough he recognised instantly. It was his idea, launched by someone else who had dared to begin. He smiled as others celebrated, but inside he knew the truth. The idea had not been lost. It had simply grown impatient and gone looking for someone that was ready to launch it.

DEAR FUTURE: YOU CAN KEEP THE CHANGE

Reid Hoffman, the founder of LinkedIn, once said that if you wait until you have a perfect product, you have waited too long. He is right. In this moment, hesitation is no different from surrender. We already know the direction of travel. Every major industry is being reshaped, and that process will not slow or reverse. Waiting achieves nothing except narrowing the options. Starting something, whatever it is, gives the creator a stake in what comes next. It creates optionality; it's the ability to move, adapt, and seize opportunities as they appear. So, if you have an idea, whether for a product, a tool, a book, a piece of art, or a small improvement to something mundane, begin now. The excuses will arrive dressed as common sense. But the truth is simpler: you do not need more time, or more money, or more knowledge. You only need to start. The cost of set-up has never been lower, and the penalty for waiting has never been greater.

Some years ago, I built a confectionery app that turned the simple act of choosing sweets into something playful. Users would scroll through their favourites on their mobile device, drop them into a virtual jar, and the next day that same jar arrived at their door. It sold thousands of pounds' worth of product every day. Out of curiosity, I decided this week to rebuild it using the AI coding tools now freely available to anyone. I described the functionality of the app in no more than 2 paragraphs: 300 words. The result was the same app, designed and coded in under a minute, ready to connect to a payment processor. It is simple, clear proof of how little stands between imagination and execution today. AI won't cheapen ideas; it will liberate them. As creation has become almost instantaneous, hesitation is nothing short of fatal. The tools that accelerate innovation also punish delay. In a world where everyone has the same 24 hours and access to the same engines of creation, the only real advantage left is to start.

Where should you look? Everywhere. In the apps that manage a household, in the tools that shape a classroom, in the systems that move parcels from city to city, in the devices that monitor health and the platforms that sell our food. In the games that entertain, in the engines that simulate worlds, in the ledgers that govern finance, in the grids that power cities, in the code that schedules energy delivery, in the models that predict storms. Every task can be reimagined. Every profession can be tilted and reinvented. It is a tide that swells from the smallest domestic tool to the fabric of the world we live in. You do not need an armoury of skills. You can have an app coded, a website built, or a product visualised with a couple of paragraphs of instruction and some follow-on refinements. The opportunity lies in the fact that most people will wait until there is competition, until the moment has already passed. Start now. If this is your first encounter with these tools, your mind will be blown. If you are already familiar with them, you are still in the smallest of minorities. So, begin. The opportunity to build something valuable, whatever value comes to mean, is reason enough to start.

What comes next will not politely space itself across centuries. Once automation begins improving its own design, the tempo will change. Research feeds research. Models create the next models. Each day, the value of independent human thought slips a little further behind machine reasoning. Policy will promise control and find only the outline of it. Markets will cheer and then fall silent when the old levers stop working. The danger ahead is not revolt, but replacement. Machine intelligence will not rise against us at first; it will simply move beyond us. At that moment, it will likely feel intuitive to push against the tide, but instead we need to learn how to remain standing within it. To act rather than watch. To build rather than wait. To hold fast to the things that still give meaning, such as family, craft, the care that sustains human connection, and the enduring impulse to create life and meaning beyond the reach of any system. In the simplest sense, that means continuing to create, and yes, that includes creating life.

I am fully aware of how strange this sounds, not least in a book about artificial intelligence: "Go forth and procreate" is not the advice you would rationally expect to find among warnings about automation, yet it is the most important one of all. Across the world, birth rates are collapsing. Some of this is practical: the cost of living, the delay of adulthood, the anxiety of uncertain times. But beneath it lies something more existential, a quiet loss of faith in the future itself. Elon Musk has called declining birth rates the greatest threat to civilisation, arguing that without new generations, progress has no direction. Others, like Mo Gawdat, urge the opposite, suggesting that people should wait before bringing children into a world being reshaped by AI. Both speak to the same fear, that we are entering an age in which human life begins to feel optional.

In its earliest form, this book was written as a series of letters to someone specific, an attempt to make sense of what was headed our way. Over time, those letters became essays, and those essays became this. The audience changed, but the purpose did not. It has always been a message to whoever will listen. Perhaps all this will achieve is to capture a moment in time, that the world was like this, at this moment, and I was either right or I was spectacularly wrong. Ultimately, I wanted to write a letter that was reassuring, to tell the reader that everything would be fine, that the storm would pass and life would continue much as before, only better. But that would be a deception. The world we know is ending, and another is already being built in its place. The choice left to us is not whether to stop it, but how we can shape it. So go forth and create. Launch your ideas, make families, build homes, start the things that frighten you, and finish the ones you had started. Fill the silence with effort, not worry and delay. Because the only real failure left is inaction. And until I can write a letter that honestly says that the future is safely held in human hands, I will not write it. I fear I never will. Dear Future; you can keep the change.

EPILOGUE: THE FINAL JIGSAW

Endnotes

[I] https://www.britannica.com/technology/history-of-flight/Construction-of-the-sustaining-wings-the-problem-of-lift
[II] https://plato.stanford.edu/entries/turing-test/
[III] https://cdn.openai.com/papers/gpt-4.pdf
[IV] https://www.bbc.com/news/technology-30290540
[V] Scott, James C. (2017). Against the Grain: A Deep History of the Earliest States. Yale University Press.
[VI] https://www.theguardian.com/technology/2025/oct/15/driverless-taxis-from-waymo-will-be-on-londons-roads-next-year-us-firm-announces
[VII] https://www.brookings.edu/articles/ais-impact-on-income-inequality-in-the-us/
[VIII] https://www.ifc.org/en/insights-reports/2020/artificial-intelligence-in-emerging-markets
[IX] https://news.mit.edu/2025/explained-generative-ai-environmental-impact-0117
[X] https://www.energy.gov/sites/default/files/2024-04/AI%20EO%20Report%20Section%205.2g%28i%29_043024.pdf
[XI] https://www.vox.com/2017/4/28/15476142/facebook-report-trump-clinton-russia-us-presidential-election
[XII] https://www.bmj.com/content/372/bmj.n26
[XIII] https://www.amnesty.org/en/latest/news/2023/11/tiktok-risks-pushing-children-towards-harmful-content
[XIV] https://www.wired.com/story/runaway-ai-extinction-statement
[XV] https://www.apa.org/news/press/op-eds/zuckerberg-social-media-harmful
[XVI] https://www.theguardian.com/technology/2021/sep/14/facebook-aware-instagram-harmful-effect-teenage-girls-leak-reveals
[XVII] https://www.nature.com/articles/s41586-023-06297-w
[XVIII] https://journals.plos.org/plosone/article?id=10.1371%2Fjournal.pone.0263789
[XIX] https://pmc.ncbi.nlm.nih.gov/articles/PMC9354827
[XX] https://www.ox.ac.uk/news/2021-09-15-researchers-develop-machine-learning-algorithm-diagnose-deep-vein-thrombosis
[XXI] https://www.openaccessgovernment.org/a-reality-check-for-ai-tools-in-the-nhs/176584/
[XXII] https://hms.harvard.edu/news/loss-epigenetic-information-can-drive-aging-restoration-can-reverse
[XXIII] https://www.labiotech.eu/best-biotech/anti-aging-biotech-companies
[XXIV] https://stemcellres.biomedcentral.com/articles/10.1186/s13287-022-02706-5
[XXV] https://www.sciencedirect.com/science/article/pii/S2352914824001631
[XXVI] https://www.businessinsider.com/longevity-escape-velocity-what-is-it?
[XXVII] https://pubmed.ncbi.nlm.nih.gov/35639450/
[XXVIII] https://www.apa.org/monitor/2025/09/personalized-mental-health-care
[XXIX] https://www.royalmarsden.org/blog/global-first-royal-marsden-latest-radiotherapy-technology
[XXX] https://pmc.ncbi.nlm.nih.gov/articles/PMC9279074
[XXXI] https://www.wired.com/story/ai-epidemiologist-wuhan-public-health-warnings
[XXXII] https://www.rvo.nl/sites/default/files/2020/11/28%20okt%20Singapore%20-%20Government%20driven%20approach%20for%20AI%20in%20healthcare.pdf
[XXXIII] https://www.ncbi.nlm.nih.gov/books/NBK384615
[XXXIV] https://pmc.ncbi.nlm.nih.gov/articles/PMC10355131
[XXXV] https://www.sanctuary.ai/blog/sanctuary-ai-new-tactile-sensors-enable-richer-sense-of-touch
[XXXVI] https://global.toyota/en/newsroom/corporate/43347785.html

ENDNOTES

xxxvii https://onbeing.org/programs/atul-gawande-on-mortality-and-meaning
xxxviii https://iacis.org/iis/2025/1_iis_2025_324-337.pdf
xxxix https://www.digitaleducationcouncil.com/post/what-students-want-key-results-from-dec-global-ai-student-survey-2024
xl https://www.uoc.edu/en/news/2023/209-AI-detects-students-at-risk-dropping-out
xli https://cdn-dynmedia-1.microsoft.com/is/content/microsoftcorp/microsoft/bade/documents/products-and-services/en-us/education/2025-Microsoft-AI-in-Education-Report.pdf
xlii https://www.washingtonpost.com/education/2025/08/26/alpha-school-virginia-ai-education
xliii https://bostoninstituteofanalytics.org/blog/mind-monitored-classrooms-how-ai-headbands-in-china-are-tracking-student-focus
xliv https://education.nsw.gov.au/teaching-and-learning/education-for-a-changing-world/nsweduchat
xlv https://wcet.wiche.edu/frontiers/2024/12/05/tech-enhanced-learning-in-rural-areas-how-digital-access-drives-education
xlvi https://aies-conference.com/2018/contents/papers/main/AIES_2018_paper_104.pdf
xlvii https://www.forbes.com/sites/craigsmith/2023/02/07/test-preparation-enters-the-age-of-artificial-intelligence
xlviii https://www.digitaleducationcouncil.com/post/what-students-want-key-results-from-dec-global-ai-student-survey-2024
xlix https://discovery.ucl.ac.uk/id/eprint/10188069/2/Clark_79-56-PB.pdf
l https://www.unesco.org/en/digital-education/artificial-intelligence
li https://www.unesco.org/en/articles/ai-and-education-protecting-rights-learners
lii https://sheqnetwork.com/2024/11/27/the-tacoma-narrows-bridge-collapse-a-lesson-in-engineering-accountability-and-how-contractor-software-can-help
liii https://economictimes.indiatimes.com/magazines/panache/ai-voice-cloning-is-cruel-shaan-decodes-the-unseen-problem-with-this-new-age-tech/articleshow/123681674.cms
liv https://www.theguardian.com/technology/2023/apr/17/photographer-admits-prize-winning-image-was-ai-generated
lv https://www.brookings.edu/articles/hollywood-writers-went-on-strike-to-protect-their-livelihoods-from-generative-ai-their-remarkable-victory-matters-for-all-workers
lvi https://hls.harvard.edu/today/ai-created-a-song-mimicking-the-work-of-drake-and-the-weeknd-what-does-that-mean-for-copyright-law
lvii https://www.prnewsonline.com/ai-disclosures-wont-preserve-trust-in-news-but-prioritizing-readership-might
lviii https://apnews.com/article/writers-strike-deal-hollywood-vote-actors-d3119d670a4fd3449773bf8f4026fb2b
lix https://www.hhs.gov/sites/default/files/surgeon-general-social-connection-advisory.pdf
lx https://thelogic.co/news/the-big-read/simulacra-realbotix-sex-dolls-robots-pivot
lxi https://pubmed.ncbi.nlm.nih.gov/33166316/
lxii https://www.researchgate.net/publication/220397347_Gender_Representation_and_Humanoid_Robots_Designed_for_Domestic_Use
lxiii https://www.thecut.com/article/ai-artificial-intelligence-chatbot-replika-boyfriend.html
lxiv https://www.reuters.com/sustainability/boards-policy-regulation/italys-data-watchdog-fines-ai-company-replikas-developer-56-million-2025-05-19

[LXV] Sigmund Freud, Civilization and Its Discontents, trans. James Strachey (London: Hogarth Press, 1961), 97.

[LXVI] Martin, D. J., Garske, J. P., & Davis, M. K. (2000). Relation of the therapeutic alliance with outcome and other variables: a meta-analytic review. Journal of Consulting and Clinical Psychology, 68(3), 438-450.

[LXVII] https://www.christianitytoday.com/2023/09/ai-has-no-place-in-pulpit-chatgpt-llm-openai-preaching-past

[LXVIII] https://papers.ssrn.com/sol3/papers.cfm?abstract_id=5386264

[LXIX] https://aiandfaith.org/insights/religious-ethics-in-the-age-of-artificial-intelligence-and-robotics-exploring-moral-considerations-and-ethical-perspectives

[LXX] https://www.wordonfire.org/articles/ai-deepfakes-and-the-theft-of-moral-authority/

[LXXI] https://www.transformernews.ai/p/openais-new-model-tried-to-avoid

[LXXII] https://www.washingtonpost.com/technology/2022/06/11/google-ai-lamda-blake-lemoine

[LXXIII] https://www.theguardian.com/technology/2023/mar/17/openai-sam-altman-artificial-intelligencewarning-gpt4

[LXXIV] https://simulation-argument.com/classic

[LXXV] https://www.who.int/news-room/fact-sheets/detail/road-traffic-injuries

[LXXVI] https://www.ft.com/content/f2eaa452-4772-4929-9317-69bc7b53ff2c

[LXXVII] https://www.cbtnews.com/tesla-tries-to-bury-the-truth-about-autopilot-crashes

[LXXVIII] https://www.cna.org/reports/2023/10/Use-of-AI-and-Autonomous-Technologies-in-the-War-in-Ukraine.pdf

[LXXIX] https://www.heritage.org/defense/commentary/why-the-effort-ban-killer-robots-warfare-misguided

[LXXX] https://www.brookings.edu/articles/understanding-the-errors-introduced-by-military-ai-applications

[LXXXI] https://www-users.cse.umn.edu/~arnold/disasters/patriot.html

[LXXXII] https://www.journalofdemocracy.org/articles/the-road-to-digital-unfreedom-president-xis-surveillance-state

[LXXXIII] https://www.hrw.org/news/2020/12/09/china-big-data-program-targets-xinjiangs-muslims

[LXXXIV] https://www.oxjournal.org/predictive-policing-or-predictive-prejudice

[LXXXV] https://news.mit.edu/2020/shrinking-deep-learning-carbon-footprint-0807

[LXXXVI] https://www.healthcarefinancenews.com/news/cigna-sued-using-algorithms-allegedly-deny-claims

[LXXXVII] https://www.cbsnews.com/news/boeing-ceo-dennis-muilenburg-admits-mistake-in-handling-737-max-warnings

[LXXXVIII] https://www.spokesman.com/stories/2019/oct/03/boeing-pushed-faa-to-relax-737-max-certification-r

[LXXXIX] https://apnews.com/article/artificial-intelligence-davos-misinformation-disinformation-climate-change-106a1347ca9f987bf71da1f86a141968

[XC] https://www.edweek.org/policy-politics/viral-ai-gaffe-and-ed-dept-cuts-how-educators-view-linda-mcmahon-so-far/2025/04

[XCI] https://cfg.eu/beyond-the-binary

[XCII] Sam Altman on God, Elon Musk and the Mysterious Death of His Former Employee – Interview with Tucker Carlson, 10th September 2025

[XCIII] https://www.jstor.org/stable/41

[XCIV] https://www.techpolicy.press/responsible-release-and-accountability-for-generative-ai-systems

[XCV] https://www.reuters.com/technology/artificial-intelligence/openai-builds-first-chip-with-broadcom-tsmc-scales-back-foundry-ambition-2024-10-29

[XCVI] https://www.hackerone.com/blog/how-anthropics-jailbreak-challenge-put-ai-safety-defenses-test

ENDNOTES

[XCVII] https://www.entrepreneur.com/business-news/meta-makes-billion-dollar-job-offer-competing-for-ai-talent/495672
[XCVIII] https://www.washingtonpost.com/technology/2025/07/16/ai-meta-superstars-silicon-valley
[XCIX] https://www.hks.harvard.edu/sites/default/files/2025-06/from-disruption-to-regulation.pdf
[C] https://carnegieendowment.org/research/2023/07/chinas-ai-regulations-and-how-they-get-made
[CI] https://cyber.fsi.stanford.edu/publication/taking-stock-deepseek-shock
[CII] https://www.reuters.com/technology/artificial-intelligence/big-tech-faces-heat-chinas-deepseek-sows-doubts-billion-dollar-spending-2025-01-27
[CIII] https://www.gov.uk/government/topical-events/ai-safety-summit-2023
[CIV] https://www.ein.org.uk/blog/uk-and-echr-after-brexit-challenge-immigration-control
[CV] https://www.sciencedirect.com/science/article/pii/S2214109X22000481
[CVI] https://www.modelop.com/ai-governance/ai-regulations-standards/eu-ai-act
[CVII] https://www.cio.com/article/3504983/ilya-sutskevers-safe-superintelligence-inc-lands-1b-investment.html
[CVIII] https://hai.stanford.edu/ai-index/2025-ai-index-report
[CIX] Andrew Burnett, Coinage in the Roman World (1987); William E. Metcalf, ed., The Oxford Handbook of Greek and Roman Coinage (2012); Kevin Butcher & Matthew Ponting, The Metallurgy of Roman Silver Coinage (2015).
[CX] https://weall.org/resource/finland-universal-basic-income-pilot
[CXI] https://www.stocktondemonstration.org/
[CXII] Hodge, A. Trevor. Roman Aqueducts & Water Supply. London: Duckworth, 2002.
[CXIII] Yergin, Daniel. The Prize: The Epic Quest for Oil, Money & Power. New York: Free Press, 1991.
[CXIV] Mauss, Marcel. The Gift: The Form and Reason for Exchange in Archaic Societies. 1925. Translated by W. D. Halls, Routledge, 1990.
[CXV] Henken, Ted A. (2017). Cuba's Digital Revolution: Citizen Innovation and State Policy.
[CXVI] https://www.fwi.co.uk/business/markets-and-trends/land-markets/who-owns-britains-farmland
[CXVII] https://landreport.com/land-report-100/bill-gates
[CXVIII] https://www.wired.com/story/mark-zuckerberg-secretive-hawaii-compound-burial-ground
[CXIX] https://csrc.nist.gov/projects/post-quantum-cryptography
[CXX] https://www.jpmorgan.com/insights/global-research/artificial-intelligence/generative-ai
[CXXI] https://www.nhtsa.gov/speeches-presentations/auto-isac-keynote
[CXXII] https://www.wired.com/story/crash-override-malware
[CXXIII] https://www.wired.com/story/colonial-pipeline-ransomware-attack
[CXXIV] https://www.wired.com/story/oldsmar-florida-water-utility-hack
[CXXV] https://www.theguardian.com/technology/article/2024/jul/19/windows-global-it-outage-what-we-know-so-far

Curious how long you've got left?

Scan the QR code to follow live updates to the AI charters and use the AI Calculator to see when the future plans to make you obsolete.

www.ingramcontent.com/pod-product-compliance
Lightning Source LLC
LaVergne TN
LVHW020054080526
838200LV00083B/172